CURSED

The second book in the best selling
Demon Kissed Series

www.DemonKissed.com

Join over 38,000 fans on facebook!
www.facebook.com/DemonKissed

CURSED

H.M. WARD

Laree Bailey Press

Laree Bailey Press, 4431 Loop 322, Abilene, TX 79602

Printed in the United States of America
First Printing: August 2011
10 9 8 7 6 5 4 3 2 1

Library of Congress Cataloging-in-Publication Data

Ward, H.M.
Cursed / H.M. Ward – 1st ed.
   p. cm.
ISBN 978-0615508276

Other Books By H.M. Ward

DEMON KISSED

TORN

*To my children
You are crazy awesome!*

*Thank you to the
Awesome fans who loved
Demon Kissed
From the very beginning.*

PAINTING OF IVY TAYLOR

CURSED

CHAPTER ONE

A speck of pure red light shone through the darkness. I could see him. My heart lurched. Collin was on his side with one hand extended before him, like he was trying to crawl away from something before he collapsed. I swallowed hard at the sight of his appearance. His clothing was torn to rags and covered in filth. His dark hair was matted to his scalp. Deep black lines were etched into his body. It was as if long blades had pierced his flesh and the wounds were left open to putrefy. A surge of rage shot from deep within me, curling my fingers into fists.

I had to get to Collin.

If I could get to him, I could get us both out of here. But, I had to physically reach him first. My eyes darted through the inky black space. A dim, red light formed a jagged circle in the rock surrounding Collin's body before it fell into darkness. He was separated by a chasm that stretched between us. Collin groaned, and the hollow place in my chest felt like it would burst. I had to get to him. Now. But, time was limited. I had until someone saw me. And in this shadowy place, someone could have been standing next to me the whole time, and I wouldn't have known. My Martis vision didn't work as well down here, though I didn't know why.

Silently, I crept forward with my heart thundering in my ears. Crouching low to the ground, I moved towards him, stretching out one leg at a time. My eyes darted through the darkness looking for other signs that demons were near, but there were none.

Why was he alone? Did they really think that I would stay away? Did they think I would abandon him? My other leg stretched forward, as I shifted my body slowly toward the rim of the abyss. It was illuminated with the slightest trace of red light that moved and flickered like fire.

Suddenly the shadows that I called with my Valefar powers, tried to retreat. The shadows were locked deep inside me, masking the faint scent of the angel blood that flowed through my veins. The shadows jerked, and attempted to sever themselves from within, but I held them tightly. The sensation made me want to scream. I bit my lip to muffle the sound, hoping I could hold them in place a little bit longer. As I neared the rim, I saw demons on the other side. They were behind Collin's limp body with their deformed backs facing toward me.

As I slid closer to the edge, the red light licked across my face, and I peered over. It was then that I felt the bond tug sharply. I looked up at Collin. His blue eyes were wide open, staring at me. He didn't move, but the expression on his face conveyed more pain than I could bear.

His thoughts brushed my mind, *Don't come closer. He's here. He kept me alive, waiting for you. Don't come.*

I'll get you out, I replied. *It'll be all right... As soon as I can reach you, you'll be safe.* Collin's blue eyes slid closed as he lost consciousness.

My heart thundered in my ears. The shadows that shrouded me were pulling, trying to slip away from me. I clenched my stomach hard, knowing that I had to hold them in place. But I was losing. Without their presence, the demons would detect me instantly. The angel blood that flowed through my veins was limited, but potent. They would catch my scent immediately. No, I had to hold the shadows in place, but there was a force greater than my own calling them away.

I could no longer contain them. Slowly, the shadow's cold presence was ripped painfully out of my throat, one by one. As the shadows retreated, the demons slowly turned. I sucked in a sharp breath as dozens of glowing red eyes landed on me. There was a moment when nothing happened. I wasn't certain if the demons would recognize me or not. There wasn't time to think about it. The shock that held them still shattered. They rushed towards me with their razor sharp teeth exposed through sneering lips.

Fear threatened to freeze me in place, but I wouldn't let it. I had to get to Collin. There was no time. I focused all my attention on the ruby stone on my finger and efanotated. They knew I was here. Using

Valefar powers in this place would expose me, but I already blew my cover.

The sear of heat shot through my body in a single burst before I reappeared next to Collin. Crouching quickly, I gripped his limp hand in mine. There was a commotion among the demons as they tried to figure out where I'd gone.

A smug smile slid across my face. I'd made it. We'd be gone before they could stop us.

But all my attention was focused on the demons. I didn't notice the enormous shadow that had stretched above us. As I looked up, my voice ripped out of my throat in a raw scream. Massive black scales covered the beast's body, and it descended on us like a hawk, poised to strike. Four gnarled finger-like claws curved grotesquely as black blades elongated from its flesh. The winged monster descended so fast that the wind screeched around it. The beast made a horrid shriek that was amplified to a deafening volume. Between ear-piercing cries from its maw, the razor sharp claws, and the cracking of its black veined wings, uncontrollable terror shot through me.

My voice rang in my ears as I screamed. Shaking, I pulled Collin into my arms, and focused on the ruby stone in my ring. Efanotating two people was dangerous, but I could do it. It was part of the powers that I possessed from the tainted blood that flowed through my veins. If I did it wrong, I would kill us both. But if I didn't do it fast enough, we would both die anyway. The heat that proceeded efanotating blossomed quickly and licked my belly from within.

Only a few more seconds and that glorious burst of searing pain would transport our bodies away from here.

We would be free.

But, fate didn't allow us a few seconds. It didn't allow us any. As the heat licked my stomach, the beast's massive talloned paw materialized above us. The gnarled bones flexed as the serpent cried out, and slammed its massive claws down on top of us.

Sweat covered my face as I sat up screaming. My fingers desperately tried to find Collin's hand, but only grabbed air. Sucking in sharply, I wiped the sweat from my eyes, and pulled my knees into my chest.

"That's the third time that I had the same vision," I rasped in a shaky voice.

Shannon's hand was on my shoulder. She squeezed it, as the trembling worked its way out of my muscles. "The one with the dragon?"

I nodded, feeling too freaked to talk. That was the third time that I'd seen my attempt to save Collin fail. And it was the third time that I'd seen my own death.

CHAPTER TWO

I pushed back my seat as we soared over the Atlantic Ocean. Shannon and I were on our way to the Martis headquarters in Rome. We boarded the plane that morning and I hadn't seen land out the window since.

Some part of me wondered how insane it was to walk straight into the Martis compound, even if I was invited. Most of the Martis still thought I was evil incarnate. It was an honest mistake, but it could have deadly consequences. While describing me as the Prophecy One was accurate, the evil part was a little out of date. I proved that fighting next to Julia, the Regent Dyconisis, and other Martis on Long Island. They had regarded me as some sort of hero after that. Well, everyone except Julia. She still had suspicion plastered all over her face the last time I'd seen her. I was learning that it was difficult to expect a Martis to look beyond the color of my tainted mark. When she looked at me, the only thing she saw was certain destruction and death.

The prophecy foretold of a seventeen-year-old as the destructor of the world. Everyone believed that I was that seventeen-year-old. It was hard to deny since the prophecy was a painting and not just words scratched onto a sheet of paper. I could have contested words, but not the painting. The resemblance was too strong. Her face was the mirror image of mine.

But, it was the violet mark on her brow that was irrefutable. That intricate mark confirmed that I was the Prophecy One without a doubt, because I was the only one who had it. No other Martis had a violet mark. Theirs were all the perfect shade of blue. Their enemies, the Valefar, had a scar scraped across their forehead that oozed an ugly red. No, there was no denying that I was the girl in the painting. My mark and hers were one and the same.

The Martis were terrified of that mark. They were terrified of me. I was the embodiment of two enemies that had been at war with each other for hundreds of thousands of years. That violet mark revealed that angel and demon blood flowed in unison through my veins. It showed the delicate and lethal balance of power that rested in the hands of one human girl.

Me.

The Martis and the Valefar were at a stalemate before I came along, but no one knows what will happen now. They think I'm a wild card. I was hoping that my actions would speak loudly and the Martis would know without a doubt whose side I was on. Being the demon queen and ruling the Underworld held no appeal for me. And, I had no desire to wipe out the Martis and destroy the world. The Valefar could go screw themselves for all I cared. I wasn't going to help them free Kreturus no matter what that prophecy said. So, my only option was to try and derail the prophecy, and hope for a different outcome. Until recently, the prophecy painting was housed safely in an old church. Now the damn thing was in the Underworld with Collin…and Kreturus.

And it was my fault.

Guilt gnawed at me constantly. I wondered what I could have done differently, what I could have changed to cause different results, but I didn't know. Collin was trying to keep the prophecy from happening as much as Eric, even though they were on different sides in the same war. The Martis and the Valefar were immortal enemies since their creation, so it was astounding that Collin and Eric were fighting for a common goal— keeping me alive. And, here I was, sitting on an airplane with my best friend, flying thousands of miles from home, to try and save the boy who sacrificed himself for me. Maybe it was the guilt that motivated me. Maybe I was stupid. Maybe I was utterly love-struck. Whatever the reason, I was determined to bring Collin home.

Julia and Eric left for Rome a couple of weeks ago. They had to report the Long Island battle to the Martis. Way too many Valefar and Martis had invaded my life. Back then, I had no idea why. Now I knew exactly why—both forces were converging on the point of the final battle. It wasn't a coincidence at all. It was me, pure and simple. The Valefar needed my power to free Kreturus and the Martis wanted me dead. Before I had any idea what I was, both sides were hunting me. Eric's sole mission for the past two-thousand years was to find and kill me.

I heard that the Martis took Eric's testimony and banished him to some remote location for his disobedience. Julia was the only one who knew his whereabouts. It seemed they wanted to make sure I didn't go looking for him. But, I couldn't. The knowledge that he was involved in my sister's death ignited something within me. It burned in my bones, and made me insane with rage if I thought about it too long. I pushed the thought away, and stared out the little oval window. The topsides of fluffy white clouds passed beneath the jumbo jet. I leaned my head against the glass.

Shannon spoke to the back of my head. She had wanted to tell me something since they closed the plane door. "The Tribunal wants me to testify as soon as we get there. Once I do that, I can help you search the library for the stuff you're looking for."

I nodded, waiting for more. But, she said nothing else.

She pulled her feet up onto her little coach class seat, and wrapped her arms around her legs. The passengers around us were sleeping. "You wanna talk?"

No. I didn't want to talk. Instead, I shrugged, and said, "There's nothing to say." I turned back toward the window. Hollowness consumed me. I hadn't spoken of Collin or my mother to anyone. I couldn't. It was too horrible.

"There's lots to say," she replied. "You just don't want to." I didn't turn to look at her. I wasn't having this conversation in an airplane, but Shannon didn't drop it. "Do you love him?"

Turning slowly, I felt my jaw open slightly in surprise. Why would she ask me that? It was like stabbing me in the heart. Of course I loved him. I finally said, "I don't want to talk about it."

She tilted her head back, examining the overhead storage bin above her as she spoke. "You used to say there was no such thing as love. Remember that?" I nodded. I believed that whole-heartedly until rather recently. "We both said that. True love was the stuff they stuck in fairytales and myths."

"It is," I replied. And I still believed for the most part that it was. True love doesn't have happy endings. Case in point; I'm on a plane and Collin is in Hell.

"Then, why won't you say that you love him?" she asked. "Ivy, he gave his life for you. He took your place in Hell. Even if you don't know how you feel, it's clear that he didn't want to be just friends."

Tears were welling up behind my eyes. She picked the worst thing to possibly talk about. I had to cut her off before I started saying things that I didn't want to share. Our relationship wasn't like it had been before I was turned into the Prophecy One. I couldn't tell her everything anymore. Loving Collin wasn't just a personal issue; it also had deadly ramifications. He was the anchor that was luring me toward the Valefar side of the war, whether I liked it or not. And I knew that Shannon didn't like that at all. Refusing to discuss it, I said, "It doesn't matter now anyway. I'm here. He isn't."

Shannon was quiet for a moment. I could feel her eyes on the side of my face, but I wouldn't look at her.

She didn't have to know everything about me. The truth was simple. The idea of loving Collin scared me to death. I'd rather go to Hell, than admit that I loved him. To anyone. Myself included. There's something eternal about love and once it starts, it doesn't stop. There is no controlling it—love does what it wants when it wants. That was dangerous enough without the prophecy.

The flight attendant asked us if we needed anything, snapping me out of my thoughts. I grabbed a blanket and Shannon requested a Coke.

After she cracked open the can, Shannon started telling me about the Martis villa in Rome. "After I testify before the Tribunal, I can help you look through the archives. We can figure something out. And that's the best place to look."

I nodded. We'd gone over this with Al in New York. The Martis had archives dating back to the beginning of time. If I was going to learn anything about Kreturus, it would be there. I just wasn't certain what I was looking for. I didn't expect them to keep documents on how to kill the ancient demon, especially since they didn't kill him themselves.

Why did they trap him, anyway? It would have been better if they killed Kreturus. Then we wouldn't be frantic worrying that he was trying to bust out of his hole in the ground—that's assuming he's still stuck. Al thought that Kreturus was no longer bound in the pit that the Martis trapped him in millennia ago. There were several reasons she was skeptical. And the demon was smart enough not to announce his escape if he was able to roam the Underworld. The rest of the Martis were walking around thinking they just had to handle the Valefar, not even thinking that their master was loose again. They could be in for a rude surprise.

Finally, I turned back towards my friend. Or frienemy. Or whatever she was, and decided to talk about things that were safe. "Tell me about the Tribunal," I said. "Is it a single person, a panel, or what?"

I leaned back in my seat and looked at her. For the first time I noticed the weary appearance of her eyes. Maybe she took all this stuff harder than I thought. There was a burden on her that I didn't notice before. Her normal lighthearted banter and carefree mannerisms were slothified. I was so wrapped up in my own grief that I hadn't noticed.

She smiled, sipped her Coke, and then said, "The Tribunal is a bunch of people. It's kind of like the Supreme Court in that they all get a say. Select Martis of each division are given a vote. They listen to testimony, and consider the words of their fellow Martis—but they are not bound to anyone or anything. They are the highest level of judges amongst us.

"The Tribunal only comes together when something is majorly screwy. Like this. Overturning a prophecy is major stuff. Al wants them to uncondemn you. Until they do, you have to worry about a Martis stabbing a silver blade in your back." She threw her head back and chugged more Coke.

"So, that's what they started? A hearing to see if I'm not evil?" I bristled.

"Nah," she said. "It's more than that. It's to see if they misunderstood the prophecy, and what their place in it was for all these years. Several very weird things happened. You being tainted in the first place and surviving a demon kiss was odd. Then, a Valefar protected you. That was unheard of. I know you and Eric hate each other right now, but you two worked together to close the portal. It looks like the Valefar and Martis are working together." She arched an eyebrow at me. "That would be super weird."

"Only if the people involved were truly Valefar. I'm not. I have a soul. And, so does Collin. That was why his actions were so erratic. Why would they think anything else?"

Some things seemed so obvious to me, but when it came to convincing the Martis of that it was difficult. I thought Eric was going to kill me when he found out that I was tainted with demon blood. Their vengeance borders on insane. Eric knew me well enough to know that I wasn't some evil, demon-aspiring wanna-be, but he couldn't see past my demon blood. That's all any of them focus on—blood. And mine's the wrong kind.

She shrugged. "They need proof. That's why they want my testimony. They'll want yours too."

What? She never said anything about having to address the Tribunal. I was supposed to tag along and research Kreturus, not waste time defending myself. I bristled and opened my mouth to speak, but she talked over me. "Ivy, you were there. You're the main person who can defend your actions. You really want someone else to do it?"

Suddenly I didn't think Shannon had been entirely truthful. Friggin Martis. They always did what they thought was best and filled you in later. I was sitting on a plane with her because she said come. If she extended the same amount of trust to me that I gave her, I would have heard of her intentions much earlier.

CHAPTER THREE

The flight took too long. I hated being stuck in a ton of tin hurling through the sky, but it was a necessary evil. Shannon didn't know I could efanotate, so I had to take the plane. We were fairly quiet the rest of the flight. When the plane finally landed in Rome, I felt a little better. Shannon and I grabbed our stuff, and walked off the aircraft with the rest of the passengers. As we left the gate and headed towards the baggage claim I noticed a few people. They didn't stick out because they failed to blend in. No, they blended with the crowds perfectly. Everything from their traveling clothes, to carry-on bags, to the travel-swept look said they were passengers from my flight. But, something was off about them. They hung back in the crowd, blending in flawlessly. I wouldn't have noticed them at all, except that I'd stopped abruptly when I fumbled my purse. It slipped out of my grasp, and toppled over my hands, landing on the floor. I ducked to grab it before a shoe kicked my bag away. Between hundreds of legs, I saw them.

"What is it?" Shannon asked.

I snatched up my purse, and stood slowly. The three had stopped moving, and they acted oddly, no longer moving with the flow of the crowd. Each one of them stopped, turned, or stooped nearly in unison. The movements were perfectly coordinated, as if I shouldn't have seen them at all. But, for some reason I did. And as soon as I noticed them, I saw others like them. Passengers who looked like they belonged, but something about them was off. It was like they knew each other but weren't acknowledging it. I tilted my head towards them and spoke softly, "We're being followed."

Shannon's gaze cut across the crowd. An unrecognizable expression crossed her eyes and vanished. She pulled my arm and leaned in next to me. "It's nothing. Keep walking."

Pulling my arm away, I said, "Shan. Are they following us or not?"

She glanced over her shoulder, "They must be moving towards the baggage claim. No big. Ignore them. I'm watching. Nothing is gonna hurt us." She flashed a smile at me and pulled at my arm again. Her reassurance didn't subdue my apprehension, but we walked on anyway.

After grabbing our bags, she walked away from the baggage claim saying, "A car should be waiting for us out front. Come on."

I didn't move. She stopped and looked back at me. I spoke softly, gesturing for her to come closer. When she did, I said, "Something isn't right. Look around you, Shan. They're everywhere." And they were. Men and women stood around not doing anything. They were not getting baggage, not waiting for someone, not hugging people hello, not talking on their cell phones, not looking like lost tourists…but they were clearly waiting for something. And there were so many of them. We were surrounded. They'd encircled us while Shannon grabbed the bags and I got a luggage cart. Damn it! Who were they? Shannon's eyes scanned the crowd, but she said nothing. "Oh, geeze, Shan. Tell me you see them?"

She nodded. "I see them." Her voice was faint. Something felt wrong. Wrong with her. Wrong with here. She recognized the expression on my face. Her fingers shot out and wrapped tightly around my arm. "Just walk Ivy. They don't trust you. If you run, God knows what'll happen."

"Holy shit!" I screeched. "You knew?" My brow pinched tightly as I shook off her grip and stepped back. "They're Martis, aren't they?" When she didn't answer, I leaned in and spat the words inches from her face, "Aren't they. Damn it, Shannon! What did you do? What did you do!" My fight or flight response reared up and I was having trouble controlling it. Blood pumped through my body at a rapid speed. The sound of my heartbeat echoed in my ears, as I watched them closing in on me. When I tore my arm free from Shannon's grip, the Martis swarmed.

Shock slowed me down, making several long seconds feel like minutes. Jaw hanging slack; I stared at

Shannon, unable to believe what she did. I was surrounded by Martis. She led me straight to them. And, these Martis didn't know me. They didn't fight with me, and watch me slashing down Valefar after Valefar with rage. They didn't see me close the portal to the Underworld with Eric's help. For all I knew, they were here to kill me. I stared at Shannon in disbelief. Her green eyes were wide. Her mouth opened offering an explanation that I didn't wait around to hear. The noise in the terminal faded until all I could hear was the lub-dub of my heart.

My finger rubbed my ruby ring, as I considered using my Valefar powers to get out of there. The Martis didn't know that I channeled my dark powers through the ruby stone in my ring. They didn't know that I had to because I wasn't a full Valefar. Collin never used a ruby to use his powers, but I had to. Rubies could contain dark magic, and that was exactly what I did with mine. I called the dark powers into the stone. The angel blood that flowed through my veins wouldn't allow the dark powers to flow directly through me, so Collin taught me to channel them through the red stone.

While dark magic was innate for the Valefar, it wasn't for me. I needed that ring. And I wasn't about to blow my secret so the Martis could take it from me. No, I'd wait until the axe dropped to use those powers—until there was no way out, and it was my only option.

Without another thought, I took off, running as fast as I could. I narrowly passed through two Martis and ran out the door. Warm air blasted my face. I didn't know where I was or where to run. There was no time to decide. Martis pursued me like I was an escaped convict. Shannon chased after me, yelling for me to stop. But I didn't. One foot slammed in front of the other. A car almost clipped me when I ran out into traffic and the light changed. The Martis were forced to wait or find another way around. A parking garage was dead ahead. I ran for it, hoping to get lost in the shadows and escape before anyone could find me.

The cars were packed into the tiny spaces like sardines. It was the parking garage with the best lighting that I'd ever seen. There were no shadows to disappear into. There was nowhere to hide. Crap!

I sprinted for the end of the row, wedging myself between parked cars before dashing up to the next level. When Martis poured out of the woodwork like roaches, I realized I was screwed.

Efanotate or let them take me.

Those were my only options. I abruptly stopped running and turned in a slow circle, surrounded. I held my palms up toward them in a universal sign for surrender, breathless.

Shannon's shoes smacked the pavement as she ran up behind the group and shouldered her way to me. "What's wrong with you? When I said *don't run*, exactly what did you think I meant?" I glared at her. "Oh, don't look at me like that. You woulda never come if I told you they wanted your testimony. It's for your own good. Now wipe that look off your face. We're still doing all the stuff I said. Julia just didn't want to risk you running off, so she sent some Martis."

Ironically, I ran because we were surrounded by Martis. "It feels like you lied to me."

She shrugged and turned away from me, "I didn't lie. I spoke the truth—literally. I wanted you to come along with me and Julia will give you access to the archives. I left out all the details and you know why. There was no way you would have come if I told you everything."

"Why don't you try it next time and let me decide?" I glared at her.

While Martis were bound to speak the truth, I was learning that it didn't mean that they couldn't lie. There were many ways to lie without saying something that wasn't true. I was learning that the hard way.

Part of me wanted to strangle Shannon. Part of me wondered what I would have done if I was her. Would I have lied to get her on a plane if I thought it was for her own good?

Probably.

The Martis surrounding me were tense waiting to see what I would do. Al told me not to piss anyone off since the prophecy was yet to be overturned. They could still kill me and be within their legal grounds to get away with it. No doubt that was what Julia was hoping for. She hates me. The Martis closed in tightly and shoved Shannon and me into a waiting car.

"That was a shitty thing to do," I spit through my teeth. "You should have told me."

"I did," she answered. "On the plane. I didn't know Julia was sending a bunch of Martis. She only told me to make sure you stayed with me and didn't run. And what did you do?" She slouched back into the seat. "You're such an idiot sometimes."

Anger surged through me. "I'm an idiot? You don't get it, do you? I'm not one of you. These people aren't my friends. Damn Shannon, it'd be like if I invited you to come with me and then surrounded you with

Valefar. Saying *it's okay, don't run* doesn't exactly instill confidence. You would have done the same thing I did. Or tried to kill all of them." My arms were folded tightly across my chest. I stared out the tinted window. We didn't speak again until we arrived at the Martis compound.

CHAPTER FOUR

The Martis villa was in an ancient section of the city, mixed in with older buildings constructed of aging stucco that dripped with rich vegetation in a rainbow of colors. The front of the Martis building looked like the structures surrounding it, but it was actually very different. It wasn't the large family home that it appeared to be from the street. It was a sprawling building that went unbelievably deep and wide. The interior of the building was impossibly large. There was no way the vast space should be able to fit inside a tiny house, but it did. And from the looks of it, we were in a palace, not a little home.

We entered through the front gates. The Martis unlocked the doors and ushered us past guards. We stopped in the foyer. It was the grandest room I'd ever been inside. Everything was doused in white light, making the room seem cheerful, but its size made it intimidating. The ivory ceiling stretched high above us with a domed recess that had a large round opening, revealing the midday sun. It looked like a pane of glass should have been in the circle, but I was certain that it was empty. There was cold white stone beneath my feet, polished to a brilliant shine. Gas lamps on ornate golden perches flickered in the corners of the room. There were works of art that adorned every whitewashed wall. Everything looked perfectly white, bright, and airy. The villa was like a terrarium encased in glass, pretty and protected.

Heels clicked against the stone floor, echoing through the space announcing her presence before I saw her. Julia. She looked like the personification of perfection. Her white pencil-skirt hugged her hips and tapered delicately at her knee. A white linen blouse with a collar that screamed designer accentuated her ample curves. The solid white ensemble was something only models and movie stars could pull off, but on her it looked perfect. Her dark hair was pulled back into a chignon at the base of her neck.

She spoke to Shannon. "We are finishing some crucial testimony tonight. Tomorrow, you will give your testimony to the Tribunal." She glared at me out of the corner of her eye. "Eventually, they will want your testimony as well. The Tribunal will decide what you are and what to do with you."

"Nice to see you too, Julia." I said through my teeth. "I really appreciated the welcoming party at the airport. Did you really think that was necessary? After I saved your butt on Long Island, how could you possibly question whose side I was fighting for?" I heard the venom in my voice, and didn't try to subdue it. The woman hated me, even though I'd helped her. It made no sense.

A plastic smile spread across her lips. "That is for the Tribunal to decide. In the meantime, you are not one of us and you will have an accompaniment. This is not negotiable. If you resist or do anything out of line, the guards have been instructed to treat you as Valefar."

Shannon's green eyes widened, "What?" she screeched. "Julia, I thought she'd be a guest here. Like me. That you just needed her to speak to the other members of the Tribunal about the Valefar attack. There is no reason for all this!"

I glanced at Shannon, wondering if she really didn't know I'd walked straight into a house arrest, or if she was playing both sides. I bit my tongue hard so I wouldn't scream.

Valefar.

They would treat me like a Valefar, not like a half-sister, even though we shared the same blood. Even though I began my immortal life as a Martis.

Julia turned sharply towards Shannon and arched an eyebrow. It clearly said, *You dare question me?* Okay, maybe Shannon didn't know Julia's plans.

"Young Dyconisis, you will do as you are told. I did not lie to you. The girl will have access to the archives as I stated. But, at no time, did I ever say she was a welcomed guest. This matter is larger than you realize. And if you want your friend to live through it, you'll tell her to do as she's told as well."

My nails were biting into my palms. I didn't realize I was clutching my fists so hard. Julia stared at me like I was an abomination—like I was the most disgusting breed of Valefar she'd ever seen. But, I'm neither one hundred percent Valefar or Martis.

I'm both.

I locked my hard gaze with hers when I felt Shannon's fingers wrap around my wrist to pull me away. "Come on," she said tugging me. "I'll take you to our room."

Julia snapped her fingers, stopping Shannon in her tracks. Two Martis guards appeared behind Julia. She looked at Shannon, explaining, "Ivy cannot reside in the same section of the Villa as the Martis. She is not one of us. It isn't safe. She will be more comfortable in the wing by the library." She looked over her shoulder and addressed the guards, "Show her the room I selected for her. Tonight she will dine in her room. She can visit the library as agreed, but nothing else." She turned back to Shannon, "Come." She snapped her fingers twice and started walking.

Shannon glanced at me and then back at Julia. Her eyes were wide and her mouth was hanging open. Al never treated anyone like this, Martis or otherwise. Al was Shannon's superior for the past year on Long Island. Al trained her and took her into the Martis fold. I could see the shock in Shannon's face. She had no idea what she'd gotten us into. She mouthed "I'm sorry," and took off after Julia who was already half way down a long corridor.

I glanced at the guards. They flanked me, but said nothing. Their white uniforms had an insignia on the chest that I hadn't seen before. It looked like interlocking blue circles with a feather on top. The Martis here were older. Both guards were men who looked to be about thirty-years-old. Their tanned skin and dark hair made their Martis mark look like it was blazing blue. Inside the Villa walls, no one concealed their mark. I'd not noticed until Julia appeared with her blue mark unmasked, and then the guards.

"So, what now?" I asked, but they didn't answer. One guard moved in front of me and the other moved behind me. They began walking with me in the middle. "Seriously? You're not going to talk to me?" It was one hundred percent clear—I was a prisoner.

After they deposited me in my room, the guards moved outside the door. When I heard the scraping of metal, I knew I'd been locked inside.

"Great." I punched a pillow on the massive couch in front of me, and fell onto the cushions. The room didn't look like a prison, but it was clear I didn't have any freedom. Except the library.

Focus. I scolded myself. *Remember why you came here.*

It was to learn more about Kreturus and find the entrance into the Underworld. I had to save Collin, and this was the only place with the information. I needed to do it. And I'd just have to deal with whatever the Martis planned to do with me.

When I calmed down enough to think clearly, I poked around my room. It looked like a posh hotel suite with a nice bed covered in light linens and too many pillows. There was a massive overstuffed sofa, and a wardrobe cabinet that looked ancient with beautiful scrolling patterns adorning the top. I kicked off my shoes and found a marble bathtub and a sink that took a while to figure out how to use. There were no faucets, just a blue basin in a white marble room. It filled with water when I touched the blue glass. The afternoon sun spilled into the room, illuminating the space. The light fixtures looked like lanterns, flickering softly. I wondered where the switches were, but couldn't find any. While I was exploring my room, there was a light knock on the door.

Surprised Shannon stole away so soon, I crossed the stone floor, and opened the wooden door. A smile slowly side across my face. "Thank God!"

Al stood there between the guards, dressed in her black habit with her wild silver hair framing her weathered face. "You gonna invite me in?"

I stepped out of the doorway and nodded. "Of course," I gestured for her to enter. The guards didn't move. It was like they didn't notice she was there. Maybe they were just that good at ignoring me. "How did you know?" She must have learned that the Martis weren't treating me like an ally, and that they had other plans for me. That had to be why she came. Al was supposed to stay in New York.

She shrugged. "Saw it. Had a vision right after you two left." She looked around the room and whistled. "Pretty nice cell, isn't it?" Her ancient eyes cut back to mine. "So you stayed. Smart girl."

"I need the information in the library. There is no other way to get it. I had to stay." Al sat on the sofa and I sat down on the floor in front of her. "They said they want me to testify before the Tribunal. By the way they are acting; testimony doesn't sound like the right word. Interrogation seems to be a better fit. Al, what's going on? What'd you see?"

She shook her head. "It was garbled. Too many possibilities. Too many choices yet to be made. The only thing that was certain was that you weren't being treated like the girl who sealed the portal to Hell. They still see you as a threat.

"My guess is that the Tribunal won't retract their position on the prophecy. That means, this trial isn't about testimony—it's about life or death. If they don't overturn the old prophecy, they won't let you leave here alive."

I stiffened. I knew I was in trouble, I just didn't realize how much. "I can't believe this. I fought next to them...on the same side! They saw me kill Valefar! How could they possibly question my loyalty?" I sighed and leaned back into the cushions. Why was I so shocked? Martis protected humanity and their own kind.

I was neither.

"It doesn't matter how they could think that. The problem is that they do. The Tribunal is the embodiment of Martis law. They are the strongest branch of the Martis. They meet rarely, but when they do," her voice softened, "well, let's just say they deliver justice swiftly. That's why I came. They didn't ask for my testimony, but I'm giving it. And I think it would be worth pushing your visions a little to see if you can control them. You need to know when the hammer will drop."

This was bad. Very bad. "You don't think I'm going to walk out of here, do you?" She shook her head. "Why are you helping me?" All the other Martis were question marks. They would protect themselves, but Al seemed to be carving a different path. She was sticking her neck out for me.

Her wrinkled lips pulled back into a smile. "I ain't stupid enough to throw out a pie just because it didn't look like the others. Sometimes those are the best ones." She winked at me and laughed. "You're not like nothing I expected."

"Right back at ya babe," I laughed. And we jumped straight into more Seyer lessons, trying to refine my skills while we still could.

CHAPTER FIVE

"No, you have to do it like you're sleeping. Otherwise it don't work. Something with rest is tied to your visions, so you gotta try to make it happen. Relax, stop thinking, and it'll come." Al was ready to beat me with a newspaper. I could tell. I just didn't understand how I could possibly summon a vision—or if I wanted to. They were turning into nightmares, showing me things that were terrifying. I groaned and suddenly felt her magazine smack into my arm.

"Al, this is pointless," I said. "Asking me to relax is like trying to talk to a kid jacked up on Pixie Stix— there's no point. I just can't. I'm surrounded by people who want to kill me. It's not exactly a relaxing environment." We'd eaten dinner in the room, and I'd yet to see Shannon. I don't know what I'd expected, but I thought that Shannon would come and tell me what was going on right away. Either she couldn't get away yet, or they weren't letting her. Either way, I was glad Al was with me.

Al sat down on the couch in front of me. I was on the floor with my legs folded in a meditating pose. Her ancient eyes sparkled when she spoke. "I know it's hard, but if you can control your visions here, you can control them in other less than ideal situations too. Seeing visions is a power—a rare power. If you can learn to do this, you'll be able to glean more information from the things you see and I suspect that you can do more than merely see visions. Your powers aren't manifesting like a typical Martis. It's possible that you'll be able to speak to me through your visions, even if I'm not there."

"What are you saying?" I asked. "That I can just dial you up and leave a message, and you'll get it the next time you see a vision?"

She nodded, "Something like that. Visions are complex. While some are of the future, others are warnings, while others are noise. I think you could possibly leave some of that noise I have to sift through to get to the heart of the visions." She shrugged.

"So you think I can leave you a message in the noise that surrounds your visions? I don't have noise around mine. There's only mist. Thick black mist. It seals out the things around me so that I can only focus on whatever it is that the vision is trying to show me."

"Black mist, huh?" Al replied looking perplexed. "You may see things differently altogether then. We might have the same Martis powers, but they sure don't work the same way."

This seemed like grasping at straws, but I wanted to know what I was capable of, and communicating with Al when she wasn't around seemed like a good idea at the time. "Ya know, I'm never sitting up when I have a vision. It's not really sleep. It just kind of knocks me out."

She nodded, saying, "Try lying down. Can't hurt. Nothing can hurt at this point, Ivy."

She tossed me a throw pillow. Before I flopped onto my back, I tucked the pillow under my head. Now I had to wait. I closed my eyes and listened to the noises of the room. I couldn't hear any of the sounds on the street. After a while the only sound I heard was my own breathing, and the tension washed away from my shoulders. I remembered this feeling. It's the place between slumber and wake; the place where dreams feel vivid and nightmares seem real. Lingering in that relaxed mental state, I wondered what I was supposed to do. I knew that sleep wouldn't come. Sleep wasn't required anymore, but this was different.

Warmth slid down my arms and caressed my back. I felt like I was floating downward, light as a feather. Then it was black, and the sounds of the room changed. A thin shroud of black mist dissipated revealing the vision had started. Dripping water was around me, but I couldn't see where it was coming from. Moisture tickled my nose and coldness chilled me to the bone.

But, where was I? Too afraid to speak, I tried to focus on something. Seeing anything would be great. Although the mist cleared, the space was covered in a darkness that my eyes could not penetrate. I knew I was somewhere else. This wasn't the Villa. That place was warm and bright, and quite the opposite of where I was now.

I felt my way through the darkness. This wasn't the same as my other visions. Nothing came into focus, and the black mist that usually blocked my view surrounding the vision wasn't there. It burned off almost as soon as it appeared. There was only utter darkness with the constant *drip, drip, drip* of water.

I moved slowly through the space expecting to find something or someone, but nothing was there. Slowly, I followed the sound of the dripping water uncertain of what else I was supposed to do. It felt like I wasn't anywhere, lodged in utter darkness and surrounded by frosty air. It was the most whacked vision I'd ever had.

Where was I?

Following the sound of the water, I moved across the blackened space touching nothing, until I saw something glimmer in the darkness. Moving towards it, I reached out and slid my hand across a pane of glass— black glass. Its surface glowed a dim mixture of blues and blacks. Its reflection contained me and the nothingness behind me. When I reached out and touched the pane again, the glass moved under my fingers. The surface felt like gelatin—thick and cold— with just as much give. Moving cautiously, I slid my finger down the glass watching it ripple beneath my touch.

Suddenly an image began to form within the black pane, and I could see the place where the water dripped. I gasped, not expecting to see him there. Collin was sitting in the corner of a cell that was carved from stone. Water dripped down the walls, staining the rocks with colored streaks. When I gasped, he looked up. His eyebrow arched, as he rose to his feet, walking towards me with a perplexed expression on his face.

My heart raced in my chest as I put my hand on the glass and pushed. But no matter how hard I tried, I could not go through. The dark mirror had hardened. "Collin…" I spoke into the glass as my fists hit the unyielding surface.

"Ivy?" he said softly. He stood in front of me, and finally shook his head. I watched him for a moment trying to understand what I was seeing. It was the place where Collin was trapped. He'd walked right in front of me, but he didn't seem to see me. But, how did he know I was there? He shook his head and mumbled, "I'm losing my mind," before he sat back down in the corner.

I beat my fists into the black glass screaming his name, but it didn't give. It didn't let me pass. It wouldn't let him hear me. It was the cruelest thing I could have imagined. I was so close, and I couldn't do anything. What was happening? Was this the past or the present? It seemed like he knew I was there, but he thought he imagined it. And this black glass, what was it? Did the mist leave it behind?

I sat at the foot of the enormous dark glass and watched Collin for a while. All the things I wanted to tell him swam into my mind. But he couldn't hear me. My teeth bit my bottom lip as I sat there helpless to free him. Collin didn't seem hurt the way he was in the vision with the dragon. That was yet to happen. The scars on his body were few, and his skin didn't have the sickly pallor of the dead. Collin hung his head and ran his fingers through his hair. He looked up one last time when I decided I should go back and ask Al what the black glass was, and how to use it. There had to be a way to use it. When I first touched it, the glass didn't resist me—my hand almost melted into it like it was nothing more than a slice of warm butter. But it wasn't. Something I did made it hard. The pane didn't shatter under the blows of my fists. It wasn't glass no matter what it looked like. But what was it?

As I stood to leave, Collin's eyes connected with mine. For a moment, I thought he saw me. I wished he saw me. I wished he could hear me. I wished I could save him.

Touching the glass, I said softly, "You were right. I was so blind. Why couldn't I see it when you were standing in front of me?"

I shook my head. Why is it that I don't notice things until it's too late?

It's not too late. Not this time. I wouldn't grieve for him. He wasn't dead. He was trapped, and trapped people can be freed.

CHAPTER SIX

When I awoke from my vision, or whatever it was, I described the black glass to Al, telling her everything I had seen. But, in all her visions, Al had never encountered the black mirror. That made me uneasy. She should have seen everything by now. She was ancient.

That was when Al spoke the words that plagued me. "It could be your powers are not as static as we thought."

"Static?" My voice was flat. "That's a nice way for saying my powers are morphing, because I've been tainted with demon blood, right?" I pushed my hair out of my face and slouched back into the couch.

She nodded. "You aren't the same. It's foolish to behave like you are. Whether you like it or not, you have some of the Valefar's abilities. Until now, I'd hoped the Martis and Valefar powers would remain separate—clearly one or the other. It would allow you to know whether or not you should use those powers. Opening the door to evil, even slightly, could have lasting repercussions; repercussions that you don't want."

I leaned forward. "You mean the slippery slope theory? If I let a little bit of evil in, I'll slide right into a mess of it?"

"Not entirely. It's just that you should know what's behind a door before you open it." She leaned towards me, her face utterly concerned. "That's what my job is—to tell new Martis what their powers are and what those powers do. But, I'm afraid I can't help you with this Ivy. Your powers are changing and combining things that don't go together."

"What am I supposed to do when I come across something that's whacked? Ya know, when I find a power that's neither Valefar or Martis." I ran my fingers through my hair. "What should I do? Ignore it?"

Al shook her head. "I doubt that would be wise. You'll have to trust your gut and make sure the purpose of the power moves in line with your plans. What did you feel from the mirror?"

My eyebrows pulled together at the weird question. "Feel? What do you mean? I stared at the glass for a while. I tried to move through it, but I couldn't. It felt like Jell-O, kind of cold and firm."

A smile spread across Al's face. She laughed, "Not physically. I mean what did you feel coming from the mirror? Did it fill you with dread, fear, cold, warmth, or what?"

I cocked my head, not really understanding what she meant. "I didn't feel anything coming from it. It's an inanimate object—a hunk of Jell-O glass. It's not like it was alive or something."

"How do you know?" Al asked completely serious. The smile slid off my face when I realized she was serious. "Ancient things, be they good or evil, seem to have a life of their own over time. They can become something else, something that they weren't intended for. Sometimes they take on the attributes of what's around them. If that mirror was in the Underworld, you should be able to sense it. You should feel evil, darkness, emanating from it. It's possible if you had walked through its pane, you'd be trapped there with Collin right now; or somewhere else entirely. Not knowing what it was or who created it—Martis or Valefar—puts you in a very precarious situation."

I stared at Al. This news didn't sit well with me. It meant that at any time, I could be walking into a trap. A trap laid by Valefar or Martis, especially since I wasn't aware of all my Valefar powers. Collin only taught me two things, and they were powers that he said wouldn't compromise me. But there were other dark powers that were inside of me—powers that came naturally to regular Valefar. I could stumble on the dark powers and unlock them without even knowing it. No wonder everyone was afraid of me. I was a time bomb.

I started to squeak out a sound, but Al cut me off. "You'll know."

"But how?" I asked burying my head in my hands. "How could I possibly know which powers are Valefar or not? How could I know if the black glass came from my mind or was some contraption that the Valefar or

Martis made a million years ago? How can I know that? It means that I can't trust myself." I shook my head, helplessly looking up at her. "There's no way to know."

She touched my shoulder, her ancient face confident, "You'll just know. You knew to stop trying to cross the black mirror today, so you sat and stared at it. Maybe you didn't realize the full extent of what powers lurk within you, and the dark magic around you, but now you do. And if you can truly manipulate Martis and Valefar powers into something new, well, Ivy—you definitely have the powers of the girl in the prophecy."

I nodded. Merging powers of darkness and light were building within me, powers that could bring utter destruction. Great. "So, you think the black mirror was a merging of my powers? The Valefar and the Martis powers blending together and turning into something else?"

"That's exactly what I think. Valefar can call darkness—shadows. Martis can see into the future and you can see into the future. See where I'm going with this? You saw a dark object, shrouded with some power that didn't allow you to pass through it. And the image you saw in the glass could be a glimpse of the future. At least it could have started that way. But, when the two powers blend together, I have no idea what you'll end up with. Light and dark ain't supposed to mix. They're like broccoli and chocolate—just nasty when you put them together—but that appears to be what's happening with you. And until you know without a doubt what's happening, you should be careful."

It wasn't what I wanted to hear, but her words made sense. I was neither fully Martis or Valefar, so why would my powers be that way? That was why the

Valefar wanted to capture me and the Martis were afraid of me. I had powers that they've never seen before. That was true for all of us, because I had no idea what I was capable of.

Looking at Al, I wondered why she wasn't afraid of me like the rest of them. "You know, you're the only Martis who I'm certain isn't trying to kill me, although I have no idea why."

She smiled, "Different things ain't necessarily bad. They're just different. And without guidance, who knows where you'll end up. Sometimes you can fix a whole lotta mess with the help of one good friend."

I laughed, "Yup, I'm a whole lotta mess. But Al, you're the only one who can help me. What if I need you?"

She smiled softly, "That just means you'll have to figure things out on your own. I won't always be here and I sure don't know everything. Follow what's inside of you. It's stronger than any prophecy, and wiser than you realize."

CHAPTER SEVEN

Al had a lot of faith in me. It was daunting. Every other Martis looked at me with venom, like they were facing down their doom. But, Al seemed to have taken the opposite approach and they hated her for it. She was obviously the old squeaky wheel in the lot. She made her presence known after she'd seen me the first night at the Villa. After that they'd kept such a close eye on us that she wasn't able to teach me more. I practiced refining my visions without her, although I did not see the black mirror again with Collin trapped on the other side. When someone has so much faith in you, it's difficult not to believe in yourself. At the same time, when everyone else keeps saying you're evil, it's hard not to doubt yourself.

I felt lost and resentful. The Martis trapped me in the compound much longer than I'd wanted, but since I still hadn't found the information I was looking for, I couldn't leave yet anyway. Days slipped into weeks, and weeks turned into months. Nearly three months had passed and I was no closer to freeing Collin than when I started. I visited the library every day. Julia's ability to only speak the truth—a trait that all Martis possessed—worked in my favor. She lured me here with access to the ancient tomes and couldn't revoke her promise. Well, maybe she could have, but she didn't. It kept us apart until whatever was going to happen would happen.

Meanwhile, I flipped through dusty pages of ancient books looking for information on Kreturus. He was my enemy, my nemesis. It wasn't Collin as I'd once thought. It wasn't the Valefar. It wasn't even Julia. The one being that could make or break me was Kreturus. He wanted me. He needed my powers for himself. While I wasn't certain what was happing, I knew Al was right. My powers were changing. It was as if the magic took on a life of its own. I had no idea how to conjure it or use the melded magic, but I was sure that Kreturus did. I was the key to him unleashing his evil plan on the world. Without me, it couldn't happen.

The prophecy boggled my mind. What could possibly happen that would entice me in the slightest to join forces with a demon? It was unfathomable. There was nothing that would cause me to do that. There was no way I'd sign onto that. Irritation was building within me. I'd been flipping through book after book, but there was nothing in these pages about Kreturus, besides the original tale of how he was captured.

The story was interesting. It was during the last battle that raged thousands and thousands of years ago.

The demons were winning after creating the Valefar. The massive number of Valefar, combined with the demons, overpowered the angels. If the angels hadn't made the Martis, they would have lost; and life as I knew it wouldn't exist.

But, they did create an immortal army of Martis. The angels bestowed all their powers on the Martis, but they spread the powers through the people so that no one person was more powerful than another. It created a cohesive force, with massive powers when they worked together. In the beginning, the Martis did work together. The Seyers were revered and worked hand-in-hand with the Dyconisis. It was nothing like Al and Julia's relationship. Julia thought Seyers were a dead breed and disregarded Al's usefulness. There was nothing about Martis Tribunals, banishments, and hearings.

The Martis back then relied on each other to overcome the demons. Not only did they lure Kreturus into a pit and trap him there, but they also pushed into the Underworld further separating humans from the evil creatures that reside there. The chasm between our world and the Underworld was well guarded, but eventually the Martis pulled out only leaving guards behind.

The books didn't say why the Martis left. There was no explanation of the current animosity between the Martis either. I had no idea where it stemmed from. The original Martis sounded great. They protected humanity from soul-sucking demons. They moved unseen and un-thanked, and they preferred it that way. They sounded like people that I would have liked.

The early Martis were responsible for ensnaring Kreturus in that pit in the Underworld, but they didn't kill him. That seemed like a colossal blunder to me. Why would they let him live? But as I read the reason became more obvious. Trapping him in a secluded part of the Underworld was like locking a king in his own thrown room. Around him were reminders of what he was, the power he held, and what he lost. And that was exactly what the Martis did. A few millennia passed and no one thought Kreturus was a threat. The Martis around the Villa still didn't believe that he was a danger, despite the testimony of Eric and Al. The rise in the number of Valefar and the attempt to open the Underworld portal last fall didn't make them change their minds either. This wasn't a case of blissful ignorance. It was a case of deep-seated fear that was too terrible to admit. If Kreturus was able to break his bonds, the Martis were totally screwed.

And so was I.

CHAPTER EIGHT

I sat at a little table decorated with Venetian glass in the courtyard of the Martis villa with Al. The sunlight filled the space, warming me. The Martis now allowed me to wander the grounds of their sprawling estate, but the guards were always with me.

Frustration flooded me as my fingers wrapped around a tiny cup with some coffee-like drink inside. After three months of searching I'd found nothing that would help me save Collin. Despair was choking me and everything was getting to me as my last shred of sanity was splitting apart.

"Al, I can't stand this much longer. What do they need to decide that I'm no threat to them?" I asked, completely exasperated. I expected them to convict me instantly, but when they didn't I started to hope that they would see me for who I was. That was hope that I severely misplaced.

Al's wrinkled hands clutched her cup. She crinkled her nose when she took a sip, and put the tiny cup down. "I thought it would have been resolved after I arrived, but they kept going." Her old eyes were full of compassion. "Use the time to prepare yourself. I know what you're planning to do, although you didn't bother to tell me."

I feigned shock. No one knew what I was really doing. They thought they talked me out of it, but they didn't. Shannon and Al thought I was looking for information on Kreturus. No one realized that the one thing that I was desperately looking for in the ancient library, but couldn't find. My forehead scrunched together, "Didn't bother to tell you what? What is it you think I'm doing here?" A smile lined my lips. I wasn't going to lie to her, but I knew she'd never approve of such an idiotic plan. And my plan was the epitome of idiocy.

She gave me one of her sassy old lady looks. "Ivy, I wasn't born yesterday. You're not planning on leaving Collin down there. I know that you're looking for a portal. You've pulled every book, scroll, and artifact on demons, the Underworld, and Kreturus. No doubt, that is part of what's making the Tribunal take so long to decide exactly what kind of threat you are to them. They don't expect you to find anything of course; otherwise they would have never let you in there.

"Ivy, you do realize that if you defeat Kreturus, you'll take his place, right? The prophecy was clear about that. If you kill him to save Collin, you'll end up being Queen of the Underworld whether you like it or not."

It wasn't like I hid what I planned to do. I even said that I was going to get Collin out of Underworld at one point, but Shannon thought she talked me out of it. Apparently, so did Al.

I released a deep breath and slumped forward onto the tiny table. "I just want to bring Collin home." I looked into her old face, "It doesn't matter anyway. I can't even figure out how to get in. The texts said that dark magic feeds off itself, whatever that means. But it also said that any outsiders would be sensed immediately. They'll smell my Martis blood, and know I'm there the second I walk in.

"And I can't just efanotate and flash in there, grab Collin, and leave since I've never been there before. Collin said I could only efanotate to places that I'd been, or I'll splice myself in half. Al, I thought if I could sneak in, and find him—then I'd have a chance. But, it doesn't matter how hard I look, there just aren't any maps that mark a backdoor to Hell." I rested my head in my hands, feeling defeated.

Al paused before speaking with her mouth hanging open, "So that's your plan? Sneak in the back door, and hope no one sees you? Goodness girl. That's a horrible plan."

I looked up at her. It didn't matter how long I thought about it, I couldn't devise a better strategy for saving Collin. "Do you have a better idea?"

She stared at me with one of her unreadable expressions and finally conceded, "No. I don't. So, you can't use Valefar powers to get in, but you can use them get out?"

"Right. According to the stuff I read, they'll sense me if I use dark magic—their magic. So I can't use my Valefar powers or I'll blow my cover. I'll have to locate Collin on my own, find him, and then I can efanotate us out." I dropped my hands back to my mini drink, and slumped back in my chair, pushing my hair out of my face. Three months and this was the best plan I could come up with.

The old woman breathed deeply. "There is a way in; a back door that no one will see you enter—if you can get past the Guardian."

I leaned forward, not believing what she was saying. "What? Where is it?" This was the most information I'd gotten about finding a way into the Underworld.

Her gray eyes were hesitant. "Ivy, do you realize that you're doing the exact thing that Collin tried to prevent? It's also exactly what Kreturus wants. If he gets hold of you, you'll have a lot more to fear than a demon kiss. And due to the unique combination in your blood, I doubt he'll rip out your soul. No, whatever fate he has planned for you is far worse than that. He'll want you alive and whole. If I tell you where the entrance is, you'll be walking straight into his trap."

"Al, I know. I've thought of that, but I can't leave Collin there." Remorse ripped through my chest in an unrelenting wave. I blinked back the tears that wanted to fall from my eyes. "I won't throw away Collin's sacrifice, but I can't abandon him either. Not if there is a way I can get to him. Al, I only have to touch his hand and we'll both be safe." The plea was very plainly written on my face.

Her old eyes locked on mine for a moment. Despite her age, she and I seemed like we were cut from the same cloth. Our ideals held us on our paths in life, whether they were easy paths or not. "Since I suspect you'll find a way in eventually, I'll tell you. But, you must realize that Kreturus is no longer contained. He may move freely in his own domain. It's possible that he is still restricted to the pit he was buried in, but I doubt it. Not after the visions you've had.

"Ah Ivy. Your convictions will be the death of you girl. Your passion will be your demise. It's written all over your face, and yet...I can't deny that you're right. Such a loyal and courageous friend does not belong in the Underworld." She pressed her lips together tightly.

It was plain that she didn't want me to go, but she seemed to understand what was driving me to do it. It wasn't just puppy love. It was as she'd said, Collin didn't belong there.

"There are several portals into the Underworld," she began. "They can be opened like you saw the night we fought the Valefar. None of the entrances are in plain sight. The Martis saw to that. And some entrances are safer than others. The oldest portal is the one you want. It's the least used and you won't find it discussed in any book. Only the Martis who were there when it was sealed knew of its existence. When the Martis left the Underworld, they marked the portal so they could return, if needed.

"This piece of knowledge has been forgotten by Martis, but the Seyers made sure that there were always two of us that knew. That way if something happened to one of us, the other knew of its location. This information was passed down from Seyer to Seyer."

She knew! Shifting to the edge of my seat, I couldn't hide the excitement on my face. She knew where the entrance to the Underworld was! She knew how to get in! But I couldn't tell if she was going to tell me. Her brow was creased, as she stared at me in silence. If she told me, she would be one of the cogs in the wheel that pushed me closer and closer to fulfilling the prophecy. The thing was, I was going whether she helped me or not. And she knew it. I just didn't believe that I would ever succumb to evil. It was so not me.

Finally Al said, "It's in the catacombs, Ivy. Read about them. As soon as you can, go and see them. But, the one thing that you have to know is that the Guardian that we posted to block the entrance will be worse than anything you could possibly imagine. The living aren't supposed to enter Hell. Remember that."

The catacombs were ancient tombs beneath the city. Was it possible? Could I really just walk into Hell through an old grave?

Excitement was bubbling inside of me. "I just have to walk through a tomb and get past a guard?" I asked.

Al's old lips smirked, "Not just any tomb; you have to find *thee* tomb.   And there is no *just getting past* anything. You must defeat the Guardian to get through. I'm sorry I can't tell you exactly what it is. That information's been lost over the centuries."

How hard could that be? It was one guard. I'd battled horrifying things before, and I'd already seen demons. I just had to kill it. I had no qualms killing demons. And if the demon guard wouldn't let me pass, I knew I could slash through its scales without remorse.

"Which tomb?" I asked.

She shook her head. "They never told me. I only know it's in the Roman catacombs, and that the Martis guarded the entrance, even though it's been forgotten."

Across the courtyard I saw Shannon striding towards us, effectively killing our conversation. Her long hair had a reddish gleam in the sunlight. It made her eyes glimmer an intense green. She pulled up a chair and sat with us.

A smile spread across her face. "I've got news."

While I hadn't really forgiven her for the airport incident, she was still acting like my friend. She kept me company, and barked at guards when they mistreated me. She'd apologized and done everything to show me that she was sorry, but I was still leery of her, although my distrust was fading. Often she seemed to be on a personal mission to clear my name.

"Spill," I said, leaning forward. She knew everything about the trial. If I couldn't find her, she was usually listening to the hearing. After several weeks, I stopped asking for updates. It just enraged me.

Shannon was practically bouncing out of her chair. Al regarded her with a concerned look, but said nothing. "The court decided that the Tribunal couldn't judge you without a critical piece of testimony. That's what was dragging things out. Everything keeps coming back to whether or not Eric sealed the portal to Hell. Some said he did—with the massive amount of light he called. They have been debating whether or not it was even possible for him to do that, and what the effects would be with an orb that large." She leaned forward, gripping the edge of the table. "Basically, they only have you saying that you sealed it. If you did seal it, they said they have no reason to fear you. But, if Eric sealed it, your loyalties are more questionable."

Al asked, "They're going to call him?" Her eyes cut to me.

Shannon nodded. "Yes. They want Eric's testimony. Again. When they first took it, no one thought to ask these things. Then Julia banished him to some Godforsaken place. But the whole thing hinges on him now."

"Great," my voice dripped with disdain, as I dropped my cup. "My life is in the hands of the guy who killed my sister; the guy who knew me and hated me the instant he learned that demon blood flows through my veins."

I shot up from the chair and started pacing. My arms folded tightly in front of me. The guards that trailed me watched, but didn't come closer. I had no privacy. I could not react. They watched me and reported everything. When I first arrived, I thought being transparent and not fighting the guards would win me brownie points, but it did no such thing. I fought to control myself, knowing they were watching.

Al's voice was careful, "He has to speak the truth, Ivy. You have nothing to worry about. He'll corroborate your testimony, and the Martis will have to release you."

Somehow I doubt the truth mattered very much in this trial anymore. I turned to look at her. Breathing deeply, I pulled my arms tighter to my chest. "I can't stand the thought of seeing him. I don't know how someone so good could have done something so evil. It makes me think I didn't know him at all."

Maybe I didn't. The Eric I knew would have never killed my sister. He was kind and caring. He was so careful to preserve life, which is why it made no sense that he killed her. And, he was the only one who knew exactly what happened to her. Half of me wanted the details of Apryl's death, while the other half was too afraid to ask.

Al was watching me carefully. She had a sixth sense and could tell what was going through my mind. "I know that you're having trouble accepting what I saw in my vision," she said, "but Eric didn't kill Apryl. Ivy, you should speak to him when he's here. I don't think he led you to believe the truth in this case. And I have no idea why he took the blame."

I shook my head, not wanting to talk about it. "It doesn't matter anymore." I looked at the guards, signaling that I was leaving. Turning back to Al and Shannon, I said, "I'm going for a walk."

Al had an odd expression on her face. She said, "Do that. Do that and while you're walking think about how you can believe and forgive one friend, but not another."

I spun on my heel, turning to her. Her words felt like a slap across the face. "What? What are you talking about? Who did I forgive for murder?"

She smiled up at me patiently, "You really need me to answer that? You already know who it is. And you forgave him. Completely."

"It's not the same," I rounded on her. "Collin was a slave. He was forced to do the things that he did. And if he killed Apryl, I wouldn't forgive him either!" I stormed away.

CHAPTER NINE

My Martis guards silently kept up with me, no doubt adding violent mood swings to their endless list of stuff that was wrong with me. Everyone knew the girl with the purple mark was deadly. Everyone held the same prejudice that Eric had uttered to me so many months ago—demon blood is vile. It is among the most dirty and dangerous things a Martis can encounter. Valefar have demon blood. It's what gave them life after their soul had been stripped clean from their body.

But that wasn't the case with me. I had been Martis before I was turned. A Valefar nearly killed me, but Collin saved me. Valefar's aren't supposed to have souls, but he did. Collin managed to hang onto a piece of his. It was too small to make him anything but Valefar, but shared with the miniscule amount of soul left in my body, following the attack, it was enough to sustain my life. Together, with the demon blood Collin gave me, I didn't die. I didn't turn Valefar either, but I was tainted. Now, I was neither Martis nor Valefar. I belonged to no one. And the result was a marriage of powers, both Martis and Valefar, into a new type of immortal with a new mark. The discolored swirl on my forehead reminded me that I didn't belong, as if I could forget it in this place. No one stayed around me unless they were forced to. I hated it here, and wanted nothing more than to leave.

After silently fuming, I lapped the building to work off some of the tension that threatened to erupt on the next person I encountered. There were two-faced Martis mixed among the people who resided in this place. On a daily basis, I dealt with them, ignoring their looks. They smiled as they passed me, but I could see in their eyes that they held the same horror of me that the more transparent folks had plastered across their faces. Al was the only one that I was certain was on my side.

Even Shannon was a question mark. She had been my best friend since birth, but I never forgot what she said to me in the old church on Long Island. She'd kill me when I became the evil one foretold in the prophecy. Until then, she was trying to keep me from that path. As far as I could tell, I wasn't on it. I didn't choose what happened to me. It was all fate. I had no control over anything. I was in the wrong place at the wrong time; which was a classic Ivy occurrence, but on a larger scale. Now instead of being in the wrong place at the wrong time and walking into a bully, I would be walking into Hell. Maybe I did bring things on myself.

Irritation shot through me. I had to go see if I could find the entrance into the Underworld that Al told me about. It was my ticket out of this place. And it pained me horribly to feel so damn helpless. Collin had been gone for three months. Three months! Meanwhile, I'd been up here finding nothing. Now that I knew what to look for, I hoped it wouldn't be much longer. He needed me. I abruptly turned around and headed toward the archives.

I was so close to finding what I needed. Now I knew the location. The entrance was somewhere in the tombs. I just had to find the correct location and figure out how to access get inside. As I walked down the hall, like I'd done so many times before, I shoved my hands in my pockets. If I encountered a Martis while walking, the guard would close in on me, reminding me that I was a prisoner, and also showing the Martis that they were safe from me. It was a joke really, because they hadn't taken my ruby ring away. They had no idea I channeled my powers through it. I could leave whenever I wanted—efanotate away—and they'd have no clue how I escaped.

Leaving this place was beyond tempting but there were two things here that I had to have before I could depart, the location of the entrance, and Apryl's Celestial Silver comb. The Martis took it from me when I arrived, which was rather pointless since I couldn't kill them with it. They said it was theirs, for a Martis warrior, which I was not. I hadn't seen it since, but there was no way I was leaving without it. As soon as I gleaned the information I needed from the archives, I'd find my comb, and get out of this place.

I rounded the corner, and cut through another courtyard that smelled sweet with winter flowers. This was the fastest way to the library. The guard closed in on me as we approached a Martis. The woman sneered at me as we passed. Considering that the Martis were supposed to be good guys, most of them were awful. It didn't dawn on anyone that I was still human, and in possession of my ravaged soul. No one remembered that I still had angel blood flowing through my veins, and that I should have been their sister Martis. No. Instead, they viewed me as an abomination and made sure I knew it.

I stared at the Martis as I passed, refusing to let her get the better of me. I was leaving soon. The Martis wouldn't chase me into the Underworld. I'd ditch the guard, and finally be on my way to rescue Collin. It'd been so long that I was sure he thought I wasn't coming.

His blue eyes and soft touch raced through my thoughts, causing my stomach to stir. The night he saved me, and took my place, he said words that I'd never forget—*I love you*. I didn't respond at the time. I said nothing, watching him fall inside the pit, taking my place.

I suck.

I kicked open the library door, my mood turning darker. The guard scribbled something on his pad behind me. I turned to him irritated, "Oh, and you guys never get mad, and kick a door, right? You're always perfect all the time." They said nothing, not acknowledging that I spoke.

They sucked, too.

I walked into the room. Massive walls stretched to the ceiling covered in whitewash, thick wooden shelves with thousands of books and ancient texts went all the way to the top. The room was gleaming white. I had no idea how they kept everything so clean. The floors, walls, ceiling, bookcases—all of it was pristine, like it was brand new despite its age. The impossibly high books on the top shelves were so far out of reach that I wondered if anyone ever read them. Each shelving unit stretched from floor to ceiling in no apparent order. There was no card catalogue or computer to look stuff up. I had to have a Martis get me the things I needed. There was a lady assigned to me, Casey, who seemed to live here. She never went home. I looked around the room for her, assuming she was lost in the stacks somewhere. I walked over to her desk, leaned on it and waited.

After a few minutes, I slid up onto her desk to sat down. There were no cushy chairs up here to wait, and if I wandered around without her, I got scolded. Despite the fact that I loathed most of the Martis, Casey wasn't so bad. I dangled my legs off the side of her desk, wondering how long she would be. The Martis had records, books, and texts going back to the beginning of time. Or at least that was what Julia said. This vault connected underground somewhere with the archives at the Vatican—the place Julia worked when she wasn't trying to kill me. I was certain my trial dragged on because of her, although no one would confirm it. That woman hated me from day one, and that was when she thought I was a Martis.

The Martis Dyconisis knew how everything was filed in this room and exactly where to find it. The

Martis were split into three groups based on their abilities and powers. There were Seyers, Dyconisis, and Polomotis. The Dyconisis were healers and handled the law. They also deciphered the Seyers' visions for the Martis. Apparently, they were also hardwired to retrieve books in a library that was the largest I'd ever seen. It was weird. There was no computer, no file, no nothing that even had a record of which books they owned.

The Dyconisis just knew.

I heard Casey approaching behind me with her quiet librarian voice. That was something that transcended cultures. I slid off her desk and turned around, shocked at who was with her. Casey turned to a small desk across the room, holding three small books. She placed the books on the little desk, and turned up the flame of an overhead lamp. She gave directions to the Martis, and as she spoke, he turned and looked up at me.

I started at him, saying nothing, not revealing the betrayal I felt. When Shannon said they were to summon Eric, I didn't realize they already had. I felt my teeth sink into my lip, as I bit down to try and remain stoic.

I don't know why my anger with Eric didn't surface the last time I saw him. Maybe I was too shocked to notice. Maybe I couldn't feel the depth of his betrayal until now. Life is like that sometimes. You sit there and stare, blank-faced and horrified, but utterly unable to respond.

Eric turned back toward Casey, nodding. He slid into the chair, and flipped open the book, ignoring me. I don't know what I wanted him to do, but that wasn't it. It confirmed the feeling that he used me, and betrayed me. *Dirty blood*, he'd said. *Abomination*. I started to walk towards him with sharp words cascading into a symphony of screams in my mind, but Casey approached me. Her petite figure and perfectly cut blonde bob would toss me out if I picked a fight. Taking a deep breath, I calmed myself. I needed my books first. There would be time to scream at Eric later.

"Yes, Miss Taylor?" Casey asked, always polite. She dressed in pastels, always pastels.

"I need books on the catacombs," I said. The movement was miniscule, but it was there. She flinched. I looked at her round face and brown eyes. She never responded like that before no matter what I asked for.

Her pretty pink smile faltered, "The Roman catacombs? What specifically are you looking for? There are hundreds of texts about them; everything from lineage to architecture."

Oh crap. I didn't plan on telling her anything. The more information I fed the Martis, the longer I made my noose. There was no doubt in my mind that if the trial didn't turn out the way Julia wanted, then she would find something else to hang me with. I needed to think of something fast, but I didn't know what to say.

Eric spoke over his shoulder. "Bring her the oldest texts you have. She'll want all four." Then he turned back to his desk. Casey looked at me for confirmation with an eyebrow raised. I nodded, and she trotted off, down the aisles of towering shelves.

I stepped closer to Eric, wanting to ask him what he knew about Apryl's death. All the information was there in his head. The memories were trapped behind his eyes. All I had to do was ask, but I couldn't. I wanted to know what happened to my sister, but I felt conflicted. Did I really want to know what happened to her? What if I couldn't handle it? Would it throw me back into my past? I nearly lost it when Apryl died. It sent me on a downward spiral that ended in a demon kiss. The pain of losing her was too great. It left a gaping hole in my chest. The void was not filled by sobbing, so I tried to fill it with other things. Like boys. I was reckless, and made out with strangers to ease the pain. But, it didn't really work.

Nothing did.

That was what happened when I learned of her death and I didn't have all the details. Would finding out the truth make it better or worse? And how was he connected? Did Eric really use me that long? Was I so stupid that I couldn't tell who my real friends were? Yes, yes I was. The problem was that I wanted to believe he was good, but such conflicting words and actions confused me.

As I stepped toward him, the guards pressed in around me, shielding Eric from me, like they were protecting him. I looked at them with hostility flashing in my eyes. "Move," I commanded. But, they remained between Eric and me. The guards didn't do this to Shannon or Al. I didn't expect them to do it to Eric, but they did. Anger burned within me as I looked at the guards. Being treated like a caged animal was making me act like one. My fingers curled into fists, ready for a fight.

Eric turned, and stood. His amber eyes looked back and forth between the guards, taking in my expression and stance. A crooked smile formed across his lips. Half laughing he said to me, "This must be driving you nuts." I locked my jaw, staring at him. In a more serious voice, he turned to the guards and said, "You can leave us."

The two guards remained where they were, and stole a glance at each other. One finally answered, "Sorry, but we were commanded to remain between this person and all other Martis; especially if she shows signs of hostility."

Eric laughed, and put his hand on the guy's shoulder. "I'm here to testify for her. She won't hurt me. I'm her ticket out of this place." Eric's smile was as genuine as his words. He tilted his head waiting for the guard to respond, still smiling. There was unspoken guy moment, and the guards stepped back.

By then, my fists were balls, hidden in the crook of my arms. I folded them so tightly over my chest that they were turning white. I hated this place. Being treated this way for so long was messing with me. It was making me want to lash out at them. I didn't think it was right to hate anyone. Live and let live. Plus, hating people is a waste of time, but I was feeling the hate right then—for all of them. I wanted to scream, but I locked my jaw instead.

Eric's smile faded as the guards backed away to their normal positions, flanking me from a distance. "How long have they held you here?"

My eye twitched when I answered, "Almost three months." I bit off the words. I sounded bitter, because I was. Three months of searching for a way to help Collin and finding nothing. Three months of hostile stares. Three months of tears no one saw me cry. It was the loneliest, most enraged time of my life. And now the guy that killed my sister was standing in front of me like everything was fine.

But it wasn't.

His eyes widened a little, before he turned back to his desk, and kicked out the chair next to him. "Sit. Ask. I see it on your face. Someone told you."

I stood for a moment, watching him slide back into his chair. His eyes looked tired. Not the kind of tired where you don't sleep for a night, but the kind of tired that comes from within. It's a fatigue that is so burdensome to bear that it nearly crushes you flat. I know. I bore it. But, why did he have that weariness? Eric didn't look like that the last time I saw him. But then, I hadn't seen him for very long. He was insisting on telling me something that he never got to say. Julia whisked him off to some place before he had the chance.

With my spine straight, I sat in the chair next to him. I didn't unfold my arms. My mouth wouldn't work either. Words wouldn't form. The truth was that I was a coward. I didn't want to know what happened to Apryl. I didn't think I could handle it. What if his words made it worse? What if she suffered? It would shatter me completely. And I didn't trust myself to not attack Eric. I could kill him instantly.

A piece of Brimstone hung around my neck disguised as a pendant. Brimstone was a powerful weapon that the Valefar forged from rare black rocks in Hell. The dark stone was lethal to Martis. One scratch from my tiny Brimstone flower and Eric would die. While he was training me back at the church on Long Island, Eric had told me that Brimstone was most commonly made into Valefar weapons, but that it was given other deadly forms, too. The most horrifying was dust. The Valefar would grind down Brimstone until it was a powdery dust that was so fine that it was barely visible. Then during combat, the Valefar blew it onto Eric's troops. One minute the Martis were slashing their Celestial Silver through their enemies, and the next they were crying out in agony. The Martis had inhaled the fatal powder. It snaked through their lungs, burning them alive from the inside out. It was the worst attack Eric had ever survived, and it was purely by chance that he wasn't near the front lines when the dust was dropped.

Eric knew what was going through my mind. I wanted to hurt the person who did this to her. I couldn't leave it alone. And if it was him, if Eric did kill Apryl, I couldn't let him walk away. His eyes said he knew I'd kill him, but his actions said something else. Why did he send away the Martis guard who would protect him? What really happened to Apryl on that pier?

Eric was cautious, but my silence caught him off guard. "You're glaring at me because someone told you, right? That I didn't directly cause your sister's death? You know. And you're mad that I said I did it. You don't know who to believe. But, you're too afraid to ask me what really happened."

"I'm not afraid of anything," I lied staring him defiantly in the face. Why was I so mad at him? Shouldn't this make it better? He wasn't the one who killed her. But then, "Why did you cover for whoever did kill her? If it wasn't you, why'd you take the blame? You lied to me, Eric. About something that was unbearable..." I shook my head, and turned away too disgusted to look at him.

His eyes dropped to the floor. "It wasn't like that. I didn't lie to you. Ivy, I took the blame, because it *was* my fault. I was reckless in how I pursued her and it led to her death. The Valefar who said I killed her were right. It was my fault."

"You weren't the one who stole her life. You weren't the one who physically killed her, though. Were you?" Direct questions. Ask him direct questions and he can't lie.

His amber eyes settled on my face. "No. I didn't take her life. I wasn't the hand that physically killed her. But I should have protected her. You were right. She was a tourist, and didn't deserve what happened to her. I'm sorry Ivy." He glanced down at his hands, as he folded his fingers together.

I was quiet for a moment. He didn't say what happened to her. He released me from that pain. But I couldn't let it go. "Eric, did you see her die?"

He gazed up at me. "Please don't ask me to tell you." His face was melancholy, as he looked me in the eye. "It won't help you. You won't heal this time. Not if you know the whole story."

He verbalized the thought that frightened me the most. It wasn't until recently that I even realized that I wanted to live. Before that, things were in a painful survival mode. How would I manage the pain this time, especially if it was worse?

Maybe I should have just believed him, and left it alone. I blinked hard, looking away. That was when I saw Casey returning with a stack of books that threatened to knock her over. Martis were freakishly strong, but it was still an odd sight. The corner of my mouth tugged up at the display. She looked cartoonish, as she wobbled slowly towards us.

I pushed my hair out of my face and looked at Eric. "I believe you. I won't ask. Not now." I don't know what expression was on my face, only that Eric made an unexpected response. His eyes darted away, before turning to Casey. I felt like he was hiding something, and he was. It just wasn't what I thought.

CHAPTER TEN

Shannon caught up with me a few hours later, and was startled to find me sitting with Eric. "I thought you were gonna kill him earlier. How are you guys sitting here like nothing ever happened?" Her hands were on her hips and she was smiling. She looked up, noticing the guards advancing, "Um, she didn't move. And she didn't say *kill*—I did. Geeze." She pulled out a chair and sat on the other side of me.

I smiled weakly at her, closing the book that I was reading. "What can I say? We made up." That wasn't the whole truth, but it was close enough. Eric was easy to trust, but I knew something wasn't right. It would be foolish to blindly trust him. No, I couldn't rely on anyone anymore. Things would never be so simple again.

Shannon leaned forward, glancing between the two of us, waiting for more of an explanation. There really wasn't more of an explanation that I wanted to share. I didn't want to know everything that Eric knew. It was more pain, and I wasn't in a position to handle it—not right now. I would ask him eventually. But right now, I had to salvage what was left of my loved ones. Collin was still alive. I'd seen it in my visions.

"So," she said to Eric, "when are you supposed to testify? Again."

Eric looked up at her. "Tonight." His amber eyes shifted to me. "Ivy, this isn't good. I already told them that you sealed the portal. They wouldn't have called me back over something minor. Julia was irate when I left."

"Maybe you left something out?" I shrugged, feeling irritated with the whole thing. "Maybe it's nothing Eric." Even as the words left my mouth, I knew they weren't true.

Shannon said, "Oh, it's not nothing. Something has them in a huff. There are Martis darting everywhere this morning. No, I think Eric's right. Something's wrong. It seems like they already made some sort of decision."

"Let's hope not," Eric said as he stood. "I'll catch up with you after the testimony. In the meantime stay out of trouble." His brow was pinched together as his eyes fell to the floor. He walked away leaving Shannon and me alone with the ancient tomes.

CHAPTER ELEVEN

Flustered, I flicked another page. "There is nothing in here!" I slammed the book shut and Casey gave me a warning glance. A sigh left my throat, as I dropped my head onto the massive open book in front of me.

I'd been reading for hours. The sunlight had turned golden as the end of the day was nearing. Eric's hearing was in a few short hours and I still hadn't found what I was looking for. I don't know what I expected, but I was hoping it was something that indicated a door or passage that had superstitions associated with it. It would be something that was part truth and part folklore to scare people away. It had to be. That was the way they did things thousands of years ago. Since Kreturus was sealed in so long ago, it made sense that the stories and folklore of the day would point towards something. The entrance was sealed after he was conquered. But, there was nothing here.

I looked up and saw Shannon walking towards me. Her chair scraped the floor as she pulled it out to sit down. "Hey," she said looking at my pile of books. "Find anything useful?" I shook my head. Shannon glanced down at the books and then back up at my face. I wasn't lying, but I guessed she suspected that I'd never stopped looking for a way to get Collin back. She didn't mention it. Instead she said, "I'm worried about Eric. I think I'm going to see if Al can get me into his hearing. I think he might be in trouble."

I nodded my head, "If anyone can get you in, it'll be Al." Weariness was making me less cautious than I should have been. "And you should go. I have the same feeling. I keep trying to tell myself that it's nothing, and that I can leave whenever I want, but...I don't know how to describe it. It feels like if I leave, I might never come back. And it has something to do with Eric, but I don't know what." My voice trailed off. The dread that had been bubbling in my stomach as the sun set was tenfold what it had been the entire time I was there. It was like my body knew what I was in for, even if my brain didn't want to admit it, yet.

Shannon's eyebrow arched and a wicked smile spread across her lips, "You can leave?" I flinched at my stupid mistake. I didn't mean to tell anyone that. Oops. I was more out of it than I thought. Her green eyes stared at me in disbelief, "Then why are you still here?"

I rested my head in my hand and looked up at her. "This is the only place to find the information I need, Shannon. But, now that they dragged Eric back...I don't know. I can't leave. Not yet. There is something here that I'm supposed to see." I gave her a lopsided smile.

We weren't best friends anymore. We never would be. The demon blood that tainted me, although it was by accident, separated us. We were cast forever in opposite sides of the same war.

She returned the grin, "Should have known. I'll come find you after the hearing and fill you in." I nodded as she walked out of the gleaming room.

Desperation flooded me. I don't know how I knew, but my time here was running out. I had to find the entrance to Hell and I had to find it now. Tears welt up behind my eyes, but I wouldn't let them fall. I couldn't utterly fail so early in my task. I was tired of feeling like an idiot. It seemed I was the last to know, the last to figure things out, and that usually lined up perfectly with being the victim. Feelings of inadequacy filled my chest. They were so drenched in sorrow that I could hardly stand it. I was a freak. A failure. Collin had been trapped down there this whole time, because of me. Why did I let him do it? Why didn't I see what was happening in front of me? Damn it! I had to do this. I had to find the entrance. This was my last chance, and I knew it.

I pushed aside the book I was reading and opened another. I had already thumbed through this one. It was filled with ancient drawings of the catacombs. It showed drawings of the tombs in fine lines and vibrant colors the way they were thousands of years ago. Although the drawings were beautiful, they held no information that I could use.

My fingers traced over the ornate decoration above an arcosolium. The arcosolium was a grave that was typically owned by the wealthy. It rested in a very large carved niche in the wall. The tomb had a fresco painted on top to seal it depicting an ancient angel watching over a woman. Sometimes the families painted an image of the deceased or a religious symbol on the grave. The painting was a form of ancient headstone. It allowed the mourners to visit her grave, and be reminded of her life.

I flipped the page. It showed several different Roman catacombs. The frescos were bright as they had once been long ago. The colors were more saturated and nothing was cracked or faded, as they were now. I leaned my head in my hand as I looked at another painting. This one was a simple depiction of Mary. It was one of the oldest surviving paintings in Christian history, and it was in one of the oldest known Roman catacombs—the Catacomb of Pricilla.

The Martis protected the tombs, and they were particularly fond of this old catacomb. I flipped in the book looking for it. There were few words, and fewer paintings at this early grave. The Catacomb of Pricilla wasn't the largest, and it didn't house as many saints and popes. With its location so far out of the way, it wasn't a major tourist attraction like the larger catacombs either. But the Catacomb of Pricilla was on the outskirts of Rome and one of the oldest tombs in the vast underground city of graves. My finger tapped the page. I looked at the crude paintings. They were much less elaborate than the others.

That was when I saw it.

My heart hammered in my chest, as my finger lingered on the piece of information I was looking for. A weird mixture of joy and disbelief flooded my body. This was it. It had to be, but it wasn't what I'd expected. That was the reason I hadn't seen it before. The entrance to Hell was indicated with a simple red mark. It was arched over an ancient tomb. Angels flanked the red symbol holding flaming swords in their hands. The two angels faced one another, with their billowy white sleeves extending toward the other. Their swords crossed and formed an X made of orange flames.

I stared at it, hardly believing that I had finally found it. This had to be it. It had to be. The early Martis marked the tomb with the red Valefar scar. It was a symbol that every Martis knew. This message was a depiction, a painting. It was a warning to keep the Martis away. Shortly after the time this catacomb was used as a burial ground, people had hidden in there to avoid persecution. Martis may have used it for similar purposes.

It made sense that there would be a warning, a reminder to stay away. The consequences of stumbling into the Underworld weren't good. Over time the Martis forgot about this portal, and the Valefar never knew it was even there. When the Martis left the area of the Underworld that they'd won, they posted a guard inside this entrance to ensure that our two worlds remained separate. The Underworld housed the demons, Valefar, the dead, and other creatures of the night. I wasn't sure what that meant, but I knew there was one person trapped down there who didn't belong—Collin.

Relief flooded my body as a satisfied smile crept across my face. I couldn't help it. The smile lit me from within. The anger and hostility that had been building inside of me for weeks was wiped out. I wanted to dance and sing at the top of my lungs that I'd found it. I'd found it. And what that meant. There was a way to get to Collin. There was a way for me to travel into the Underworld and save him. And when I found him...the memory of his arms around me flooded me. I couldn't wait. Not another second. When I stood and swirled suddenly, I bumped into Casey who was standing over my shoulder.

I sucked in a shocked gasp and scolded her without thinking. "Oww! Crap Casey! You really shouldn't do that!" My hand clutched my heart as I tried to steady myself.

She smiled at me, "I'm sorry. I thought you heard me." She looked down at the open book. "Are you finished with these?"

I nodded, and closed the books hoping she didn't see exactly what I'd been looking at. She didn't act like she had. I thought about asking her because she would have to answer with the truth, but then I saw the time. It was seven o'clock. Eric's hearing just started.

Instead, I said, "Thank you. I'll see you again tomorrow," knowing full well that I wouldn't.

CHAPTER TWELVE

I hoped that I could find Al quickly to confirm what I thought about the abandoned Martis entrance to the Underworld. The catacombs were massive, sprawling under a large section of Rome, and if I was wrong, if I picked the wrong location, there were too many tombs to randomly pick another and hope I was right. To make my escape, it was important to have the correct grave picked the first time.

The gleaming hallways were illuminated by flickering lamplights, as the sun was swallowed by the horizon. My guard followed behind me, saying nothing about my change in mood. The hallways were deserted, which was odd for this time of day, but I suspected that the Martis were all trying to hear Eric's testimony. There was tension in the air, and it only worsened as the evening progressed.

Before I found Al, I was redirected by two more Martis guards. They were dressed in blue, and they had the insignia of the court stitched onto the left breast of their uniform. I wasn't certain what their role was, but I knew it was different than my normal guard because of their uniforms. They weren't just guards. My dual escort dropped back allowing the new Martis to move in closer.

They rerouted me through the building, refusing to answer my questions. Eventually, we neared the lower chambers of the villa and I knew that they were ushering me to the hearing.

I continued to speak to them, though they didn't reply. "What do they want me for? Is Eric all right?"

Why wouldn't he be all right? He couldn't lie, well not totally, and we sealed the portal together. Case closed.

So why all the guards? And where was everybody?

A bead of sweat rolled down my spine making me shiver. This was bad. My finger nervously rubbed my ruby ring to abate my tension. There would be no coming back once I left.

The guards walked me along the corridors to the courtrooms. We passed ogling Martis who weren't important enough to get inside the court room where Eric was waiting. I'd been in the room several times, and it was equally intimidating every time. The court room was white travertine stone, like the rest of the building. Ornately decorated bleached oak dividers encircled the center of the room. The person being questioned sat alone in the center of the floor. That was where Eric sat now. Behind the dividers sat rows upon rows of Martis. They were divided into three sections, each according to his or her specialty—Polomotis, Seyer, and Dyconisis. The eldest and most influential members sat in the first row with their Martis marks exposed. Guards flanked every entrance and exit in the room. They wore the same insignia and uniform as that of my new Martis guards.

The court felt cold, and unforgiving. Not sitting next to a judge or lawyer made the person testifying feel isolated. Maybe that was the intent. If you put someone on the stand, and made them feel utterly alone, and outnumbered by row upon row of immortals...well, it's intimidating even if you are innocent. I can't even imagine how the guilty must feel.

How do you have a guilty Martis anyway? It's not like they can totally lie. And they pretty much do what they are told. They're like a bunch of lemmings in that way. Martis glared at me as I was escorted into the back of the room. I glared back. The guards stopped me before I could enter the small circle where Eric sat. They didn't stop his testimony to get me. I'd walked in while it was still going on.

Eric sat on a small white chair with an expression on his face that I'd never seen before. His brow was pinched tight, and his fingers were balled into fists on his lap. He sat at the edge of his seat like a metal pole was strapped to his spine. His amber eyes were blazing as he stared at the Martis who was questioning him— Julia.

"Answer the question, Eric. Did you or did you not see Ivy Taylor perform a demon kiss on a Valefar to revive him?" Julia's jaw locked as she gripped the oak partition in front of her.

Eric sounded like he could barely restrain himself, "Yes."

"And did you or did you not have the opportunity to destroy both Ivy Taylor and this Valefar?" Julia was leaning forward now, her eyes narrowing. The room was utterly silent.

Eric's jaw tightened. For a brief second his eyes flicked to mine, and then stared at Julia. "Yes." The gasps in the courtroom were so loud that it took a few minutes for Julia to restore order.

Another Martis sitting next to Julia spoke out. His voice resonated through the remnants of shocked whispers, "Then answer, boy. Why did you betray your own kind and let her live?"

At that second I understood what was happening. They didn't call Eric back for his testimony; they called him back to condemn him—for sparing my life. They were asking him about a different night; a night that happened so fast that I wasn't sure what happened at all. They were questioning Eric about the evening that I saved Collin. I never would have said I gave him a demon kiss. A demon kiss rips the victim's soul out of their body through a kiss. No, that wasn't what happened at all.

That night was a flood of images forever burned behind my eyes. Eric's face contorted with rage when he saw me emerge with Collin. He thought I was bound to Collin. He thought I turned Valefar. Eric's sword swung and slashed through Collin. There was so much blood. Collin's limp body lay in my lap, as I cradled him in my arms. Tears blurred my vision. And before I knew what happened, I kissed him. I gave him my blood…my tainted angel blood. But that wasn't the craziest thing I'd done. No, I did something more insane.

And that was what the Martis found out. That was why they were enraged. Someone told them that I'd saved Collin. Someone had told them that my kiss with Collin worked like a demon kiss in reverse. Instead of stealing Collin's soul, I gave him a piece of mine—a piece big enough for him to live.

I saved a Valefar. And not just any Valefar. The leader of the Valefar—Collin Smith.

And Eric...he did nothing to stop it, which was equally shocking since he was the golden boy of the Martis warriors. Martis came from all over the world to learn from him. There was no one better than him. But, he let this happen.

My eyes widened, and I felt myself leaning towards him. Why did he let that happen? I never realized what he did. There was a second when I was vulnerable, but Eric didn't strike. He sliced through Collin, but hesitated when it came to me. I always thought that the dark mist that swirled around Collin and I had protected me. Maybe it hadn't. Maybe Eric faltered.

My opinion of him shattered. I had no idea what to think. Eric hated Valefar. He detested everything about them, and I was half Valefar. But he saved me. He spared me when he thought I was a full Valefar? What the hell? Why would he do that? Did he really do that?

Stunned, I stood there with my mouth hanging open. I had no idea what I thought of Eric at that moment, but I wanted him to stop speaking. He was damning himself. His kind wouldn't forgive his actions.

Not for this. It appeared to be beyond an accident. Sparing me was beyond a colossal failure.

It was mutiny.

Before I realized I was moving, a strong hand clamped down on both my shoulders. I looked back at the guards, and they shook their heads indicating for me to remain where I was.

Eric swallowed hard. A vein on the side of his face was throbbing, and his temples shined with sweat. He unclenched his jaw and spoke calmly and evenly, not apologizing, "I cannot say."

Julia shot up from her seat enraged. "You can say! And you will! Why didn't you kill them? You had the Prophecy One in your grasp and she was vulnerable. She proved she can create more of her kind, and you did nothing! Nothing! A new Martis stood at your side, waiting to attack, but you did nothing! Eric, you were our most trusted warrior. You pursued the Prophecy One for almost two millennia. You did exactly as commanded; found her, befriended her, but when the chance came to destroy her, you failed. Answer for your misconduct, or we will answer for you."

The sound of silence filled the air. No one breathed. Everything felt surreal, passing slower than time allowed. Mixed emotions flooded my chest. I had no idea that he pretended to be my friend. I thought he cared about me the same way Shannon had before we ended up on opposite sides. As if he could hear my thoughts he turned his head toward me. His golden gaze softened, and there were words in his eyes that he could not speak.

Not here. Not now.

The Martis grew impatient with his lack of response. Julia screeched at him, but he said nothing. The Martis guards that surrounded the room were rigid, waiting for something that I didn't see coming. When Eric refused to answer and Julia was done berating him, another Martis spoke.

This man was older, his voice softer, but no less powerful, "Eric, if you will not defend yourself we have no choice but to find you guilty...of treason." The old man looked at Eric with concern.

Behind him sat Al, and several rows back sat Shannon. Shannon's face revealed raw terror as the guard behind Eric moved slowly toward him, holding silver chains. Her green eyes were wide when she caught sight of me. It looked like she was caught in a silent scream.

Eric didn't move. He didn't speak. He remained on the chair, with his jaw locked tight. The guards pulled his wrists behind his back and bound them with the silver chain. Eric's brazen gaze did not falter. He stared at Julia.

The old Martis sighed in resignation, "Eric, you've left us no choice. You have broken our code of honor and abandoned your quest before completion. You did the unthinkable and allowed a powerful Valefar to regain life, by failing to kill your target. Your defiance makes us think that you are under the influence of another." His eyes cut to me, and then back to Eric. "Because you will not counter these claims, we have no choice but to sentence you as traitor. You are hereby stripped of your title and rank. Celestial silver made you one of us, now it will take you away." The man's face was grim, as he turned away from Eric. It was as if he were too horrified to watch.

The guard, who restrained Eric, stepped in front of him. Eric didn't move. He didn't plead, flinch or try to run. He sat rigidly; intent on taking whatever they were going to dish out. The guard tore open the front of Eric's white shirt, and ripped his Celestial Sliver necklace away. They took his only means to protect himself against the Valefar. Now there was no way to kill his enemies or hide his Martis mark.

The guard touched the small silver X pendant on Eric's necklace to his mark. The silver glowed blue before changing into a sword, Eric's sword. The guard turned, and walked toward the elder Martis with the sword lying across his open palms. He was saying something that didn't make sense to me, as some Martis handed him something. Were they speaking Latin?

The guard moved carefully, as if he were handling poison. The room was eerily silent. It wasn't until the guard turned around again that I realized what he'd done. The gleaming silver sword was covered in a black substance that clung to the blade. My heart jumped into my throat. It couldn't be. But it was.

Brimstone. They coated the entire blade with the lethal black substance.

Paralyzed, I stood there watching. I didn't know what was happening. There was no way they were going to do what I thought they were going to do. They wouldn't kill their own kind, would they? Suddenly, I wasn't too certain. Some of the Martis looked shocked, while others were outraged. But, Eric's face didn't waiver. He didn't beg, speak, or cry out. Surely he'd say something if he was in mortal danger.

Disbelief was making me stupid. The guard continued to move towards Eric. Eric continued to remain silent. If he spoke, and said why he didn't kill me that night, there was no way that this would happen.

The elder Martis made that clear. But Eric said nothing. Why was he doing this?

Everything else happened in a matter of seconds, utterly horrifying seconds. The Martis guard turned. He held Eric's sword above his head for the entire court to see, careful not to touch the blade, turning slowly to each side of the room and then back to Eric. The entire assembly was on the edge of their seats. Al was vigorously pulling at the man sitting next to Julia, spewing off angry words in his ear. But, he only shook his head. Shannon was sitting rigid with a look of horror frozen across her face.

The sword. The fear. The guard. The guard was delivering the punishment. My eyes widened as I accepted the reality of the Martis penalty for treason.

Death.

This was an execution. My mouth dropped open in horror. I couldn't swallow. My body wouldn't move. Every sound in the room faded away. I stared at Eric in disbelief. He knew. He knew his actions that night were guilty of treason, an offense punishable by death—but he did it anyway. He let me live. Me and my rancid demon blood filled body. Me. The abomination. Me. His prey for centuries.

My eyebrows pinched together as trembling worked its way up my tense muscles. It was then that Eric finally looked at me. His expression softened, as he mouthed, *I'm sorry*. His golden eyes remained locked with mine. They revealed unspoken sorrow that I would have never listened to had he tried to put it into words.

That did it. I couldn't stand it anymore. I couldn't wait here! Not another second. No way. I don't know what Eric's angle was, or if he even had one, but at that moment I felt utter hatred flame through me. But, this time it wasn't directed at Eric. It was directed at everyone else—the Martis. They were the ones who were sentencing him to death. And, it was because of me. They thought I deserved to die. Eric didn't. He spared me. I couldn't watch whatever they were going to do to him. I couldn't tolerate it. This was unjust. It wasn't right. Eric saw something in me that they didn't. His logic didn't always make sense to me, but this was wrong.

I felt my eyes rim violet, as I began to lose control of my anger. I could feel it happening. It was the same insane rage that shot through me when I slashed down Valefar after Valefar last fall. My lungs felt like they were on fire. Every muscle in my body went rigid as if I were prepared to fight to the death. The tips of my hair flamed deep violet. I could see it happening out of the corner of my eye. I didn't know why that happened some times and not others. Truth was I didn't care. I let the surge of power overtake me. The air felt like it was stifling hot, crushing my body.

I must have looked insane. Someone near me shrieked, while others pointed in alarm. My guard hesitated, backing away from me. They were terrified. I could see it in their eyes.

Now many of the Martis were standing, and screaming to be heard over the chaos. Julia was standing, leaning over the oak divider, and screaming at the guard to finish his job. Al was silent, watching me. The old Martis next to her was pulling at Julia to sit down and restore order. But, she wouldn't. Utter hatred flashed across her face when she looked at Eric. And something worse appeared when she looked at me. She knew what I could do, even if I didn't. And at that moment, I didn't have any clue what I was capable of or why I was dangerous.

I acted without thinking. I had to. There was no time left. The guard suddenly remembered he had arms. His sword swung backwards, poised to swing down and lodge the blackened blade in Eric's skull. I launched myself across the room at exactly the same moment that the silver sword swung down. The swordsmen did not falter until my hurtling body appeared in front of him. During that brief second, he hesitated making his sword falter mid-swing.

I crashed into Eric, causing his chair to rock back and crash to the floor. The sword completely missed Eric and nearly cleaved me in two. The silver sword slashed down my back ripping the flesh open. Pain shot through my body, as the tainted blade tore through me. Others were shouting, but it was too late. Heat surged through my body as the efanotation began.

My arms were wrapped around Eric, as we fell and I allowed the heat of the efanotation to overtake us. The screams, gasps, and chaos were soon muffled by the roar of fire coursing through my body. I knew where I wanted us to arrive, but I'd never been there before. And the screaming pain in my back was making it difficult to concentrate. I'd broken a cardinal rule of efanotation. In order to move your body from one place to another, you had to have been there before. Collin once told me he spliced himself, and separated his skin from his body, because he didn't observe that little rule. I never bothered to ask him how to fix that. I just knew it would hurt beyond comprehension.

As it was, no other Valefar could efanotate with another person. But, I could when I didn't have a fatal wound on my back. While Celestial Silver or Brimstone alone couldn't kill me, combined they might succeed. The demon blood that flowed through my soul-ravaged body overtook me. The dark magic coursed through my veins. Valefar powers were always paid for with pain. Efanotating felt like I was being burned alive from the inside out. I could barely tolerate it under normal circumstances. The wound on my back made it unbearable. I noticed I was crushing Eric's limp body in my arms. He didn't have any demon blood to protect him from the scalding heat. And, I knew he felt it. As long as I maintained contact with Eric, he would come with me, and feel what I felt—or worse. I risked killing him instantly and splicing us both, but I had to. There was no other choice.

The heat licked my stomach making me cry out in agony. Warm blood oozed from my back, stinging as it touched my sweat soaked shirt. *Catacomb. Focus, Ivy.* Attempting to ignore the pain, I continued to picture the painting from the book in my mind; every vivid detail. The angel's wings. The flaming swords. The Valefar mark painted on the tomb. I imagined the cool smell of the earth and the narrow passages that surrounded the graves.

I clutched Eric harder when I heard him cry out. I couldn't stop it. There was no stopping efanotation midway through. The pain was intensifying and searing every inch of my body from within. My lungs let out another scream drowning out Eric's cries. The cold earth crashed into us abruptly.

I fell face-down in the dirt and lost consciousness as the pain in my back overtook me.

CHAPTER THIRTEEN

Pain coursed through my body unlike anything I've ever felt before. My muscles felt raw in an unnatural way. I patted my arms, checking to make sure my skin was still intact. It felt like it had been fried off. That was the most painful efanotation that I've ever done. I sighed in relief, rubbing out my sore muscles, and sat up looking for Eric. He was lying a few feet from me, facedown into the dirt. He rolled onto his back and was breathing hard. Dirt streaked his white shirt.

I slowly dragged my wounded body toward him. A moan escaped his lips as he tried to move. His amber eyes opened cautiously and stared at the tomb ceiling. He blinked slowly, finally focusing on my face. "What happened? Where are we?" he asked.

Leaning over him, I looked to see if efanotating caused him any permanent damage. He obviously didn't do with it well, but he seemed fairly unscathed. He would have looked better if I didn't hurl us into the floor.

Relieved, I breathed, "We're somewhere safe; for the moment anyway. We're under Rome." In a grave. I left that part off since it was obvious from the piles of bones stuffed into the stone walls. I slammed my eyes closed and stifled a moan.

"Are you all right?" he asked sitting up.

I looked up at him. "The blade hit my back."

The expression on his face changed, as he crawled next to me. Slowly I sat up, trying hard to swallow the pain. He knelt behind me and after a minute said, "Your shirt is covered in blood, but it's stuck to the wound. I can't see it very well. May I?" indicating he needed to look under the shirt to see how bad it was.

I nodded, "Just do it, Eric." He hesitated. My back was covered in blood. When he didn't move I turned sharply and said, "Forget it."

"Ivy stop," he said. "It's not like that."

"Then what's your problem? You're so afraid of touching demon blood that you won't help me. Forget it Eric."

"No, that's not it. If you'd be quiet for a minute, I'd tell you." I folded my arms and stared at him. Bright red marks blossomed in his cheeks until his entire face was in a full blush. "The blade cut through your bra. The strap is cut three-quarters of the way through."

I laughed. "I was slashed with a deadly weapon and you're blushing over the back of my bra strap? Seriously, Eric?" I reached behind me and ripped the strings that were holding the fabric together. The bra broke, and I pulled it out from under my shirt and threw it on the floor. The back strap was covered in blood.

Eric's blush deepened, but I pretended not to notice. It was kind of sweet. "You shouldn't be walking around, ya know. From the amount of blood on your back, you should be dead." His fingers pushed the torn sections of the back of my shirt apart. For a moment he said nothing, and then I felt his fingers pressed lightly on my back, and I flinched. "Does that hurt?"

I shook my head. "Not really. But, you're hands are cold. How bad is it?" He moved in front of me. Eric's expression was odd. He studied my face and then looked at the floor, gathering his thoughts. His response was making me panic. I tried to look over my shoulder to see the wound, but I couldn't twist far enough to see anything. "Eric! Tell me."

His gold eyes looked up at me with a blank expression. "There's nothing there. The wound's gone. The only thing left is the dried blood sticking to your back." I stared at him for a moment. My finger reached around to the spot where the wound was and slid over my skin. Caked blood came off in my fingers, but nothing else. No warm, wet blood. What happened to the wound? "Well, apparently silver and Brimstone in the back won't kill you."

I stared at the dried blood on my fingertips. "How is that possible? Where's the cut? Shannon had to heal me last time I was hurt. I know I was cut badly. That blade sliced through my back. It missed bone, but I felt it slice my skin open. The pain was unbearable. It wasn't a scratch. And it's still sore."

Eric shrugged. "Part of the mystery of the Prophecy One. Martis can heal from most wounds, and so can you. That's why you didn't need Shannon this time. You're part Martis and your powers are intensifying. You healed yourself. You're changing, Ivy. You're changing into the Prophecy One." I cringed. I didn't want to be the Prophecy One. At the same time, I was still alive because I was. Eric looked around and then asked, "We're in the catacombs, aren't we?" I nodded. "How did we get here?"

"We efanotated," I said cautiously. He was going to be pissed. I used Valefar magic on him. He hated that part of me. Well, I wasn't going to hide it. Those dark powers saved our lives. I didn't really care where they originated from at the moment, but the former Seeker might have difficulty disregarding it. I decided to explain when he didn't respond. "I can make my body move from one location to another by thinking about it. It hurts like hell, but it saved us."

Eric's brow pinched together as he stared at me with his mouth open. He was frozen…but with what? I expected him to rip into me and give me the scolding of a lifetime. But the tension flowed out of him and he smiled saying, "Then, why did you stay there for three months? The Martis thought they had you trapped. And this whole time, you could have left whenever you wanted?"

I nodded as the corner of my mouth pulled into a faint smile. "Yeah. I could have left whenever. I stayed because it seemed like they'd see…Well, I was hoping that they'd notice that I wasn't evil incarnate the way they thought. But, after a while, it didn't seem like they were capable of seeing me any other way. It didn't matter what I did." I pushed a curl back behind my ear. "Then I was just staying to research stuff about

Kreturus. I spent the entire time looking for a backdoor into the Underworld. I planned on leaving as soon as I knew for certain, but the Martis said I was needed at the hearing. They stopped me earlier and dragged me to the courtroom. And I wanted to know what happened to you. So, what happened?"

Eric's eyes darted away from mine for a second. When they returned to my face he seemed decided about something. "They called me back. They initially questioned me about the battle and sealng the portal. When I repeated that you helped me, and said I did not act alone, they changed what they were questioning me about. They shifted to another night, night that I should have killed you, the night you changed Collin. I stood there and watched. I did nothing. Shannon was to follow my lead. She failed to act because of me.

"Then, tonight the Tribunal told me your fate—you were to be executed. They concluded that they had to destroy you before it was too late, and that your involvement in sealing the portal was irrelevant. The Tribunal said that there was nothing I could do that would change their minds, but they had hoped you would try to change mine. You were supposed to be used as leverage to get me to speak." He laughed, "That didn't work out the way they planned, huh?"

I stared at him with my mouth hanging open and a shocked expression on my face. I didn't know what to say. The Tribunal already sentenced me? Why didn't Shannon or Al know about it? And they moved onto other matters, like my ability to save Valefar, and the one boy that could have killed me, but didn't.

"Eric, why didn't you just tell them? You couldn't kill us. You couldn't even see what was happening until it was over." That night was a blur. I remembered Eric being irate, but I didn't remember him being passive and just letting it all happen.

He shook his head. "Ivy, there was black mist swirling around you, but not in the beginning. When you tried to help him, I was shocked. I couldn't tell if you were a Valefar or... you. So I waited when I should have killed you. Then after that, I could have called as much light as I wanted to try and bust the black mist apart. I didn't. I just stood there." He went to say something else, but closed his mouth instead. He looked away from me.

"Why'd you hesitate? Why not kill me if you thought I was Valefar? Eric, what aren't you telling me?" I tried to piece things together in my mind, but they weren't coming together. He should have killed me that night. No questions asked. He thought I was a Valefar. But when he realized that I wasn't, I was still The Prophecy One—the girl he'd been hunting for centuries—and he did nothing. He should have killed me, but he didn't. Why not? Especially with the rage that was plastered all over his face that night. What was with him? Why couldn't I figure this out? It made me totally uncertain about Eric. It was part of his bipolar personality. At least he seemed that way to me. He didn't do things half way. His actions were either totally saintly or inherently evil. I didn't know what motivated him to act the way he did. Without that information, I couldn't decide if he was trying to help me, or finish his original assignment to kill me.

He looked away. "Ivy, it doesn't matter now."

"Yes, it does." I bit my lip, trying to restrain my emotions. Why didn't he understand? I blinked slowly, calming myself, and tried to explain. "Eric, I don't know where we stand. Are you saying that you want to be my friend? Is that what you mean? Your Martis brain shorted out and you decided to befriend the enemy for real?"

He laughed, "I don't know what I decided. I just saw you with him—I could see you through the mist. It didn't conceal you. Not the way you thought. I saw you holding him in your arms and..." he looked away. "I thought the Martis were wrong about you. Evil creatures cannot love. The way you looked at him...the way you protected him. It reminded me of everything I lost. It reminded me of what I would have done to save her. I didn't have the chance, but you did. And I wasn't going to be the one to take it away. I decided the Martis were wrong about you. Ivy, I *am* a traitor. I damned myself. That's why I didn't speak. There was nothing to say because...they were right." He rose and brushed the dirt off his jeans. The sleeves of his white dress shirt were caked with streaks of dirt. He batted at it, but I pulled him toward me.

When his eyes met mine, I said, "They weren't right about you. You're not a traitor. You just see more than they do. You're willing to look past the traits that damned me, and see the girl trapped beneath." His amber eyes were intense, drinking in everything I said as if he were parched. "I still have a soul. I'm still alive. You knew that and refused to destroy me. That makes you courageous, not a traitor." I dropped my hand, and looked away.

The Martis were so blind. How could they not see Eric for what he was? But then, I wasn't exactly certain what he was either. I sighed, "So, we both have a price on our heads, then?" He nodded. "Well, good thing I took you with me. So, what now? Are you going to try to stop me from doing the stupidest thing I've ever done?"

His lips curled into a lopsided smile, "What are you going to do, Ivy?" I walked over to one of the tombs. The painting that covered the fresco was aged. The colors were no longer vibrant like those in the book, but the two angels with flaming swords were there. This was the right place. I just didn't know what to do.

Eric walked up behind me, "This is the entrance, isn't it? You're going after him?"

I turned, "I have to. I can't leave Collin there. He took my place, Eric." Turning back to the wall, I ran my fingers along the aged plaster wondering how to get inside. "And I can't stay here. The Martis won't stop until they have my head on a stick. It looks like I'm destined to meet Kreturus one way or another. This is supposed to be the way in. See the flaming swords and the Valefar scar staining the wall behind the angels?" Eric nodded, as he approached the grave. "The entrance is here. Somewhere. I just don't know how to get in."

Desperation laced my thoughts. I came here too soon, but I had no other choice. I didn't get to ask Al anything about this. Surely she would have known if I was in the right place and how to open the portal. She knew everything. But I was denied that opportunity. I walked along the narrow space, dragging my fingers against the wall.

Eric asked, "If I tell you how to get inside, will you take me with you?"

I snapped my neck around, "What? What did you say?"

"I'll open it if you take me with you."

"Why?" I asked folding my arms against my chest. It was a suicide mission, and he had no reason to go.

"I have to finish my mission. I swore I would prevent the prophecy from occurring the way the Martis thought. It's not you that worries me—it's Kreturus. You can't go into the Underworld alone, unprotected. And I can't stay here either. The Martis are after both of us."

I bit my lip. He shouldn't come. I should say no and send him back. He was better off staying topside and running from Martis, rather than being eaten by Valefar below.

I shook my head and spoke with certain resolve as I turned back toward the fresco. "No, I can't ask you to come with me. I have to do this alone. I caused this to happen. I have to fix it." I touched the plaster again looking for anything to indicate an opening. I needed Eric, but I couldn't ask him to do this.

He laughed and grabbed my shoulder, turning me around. Shock showed on my face, as he laughed, "You really think you can tell me no? You think you can make me stay here and hide until you get back—if you get back? And then what? The Martis see that they were wrong and all is forgiven? No. Things don't work like that and you know it.

"And what if you don't come back at all? What if Kreturus finds you as soon as you step inside? He'll catch your scent, with the faint smell of angel blood that flows through your veins. His demons will drag you back to him. That's the part that scares me. Not only do I prefer you alive, but if he gets you, he gets your power. The prophecy is about him using you. I can't let you go alone." He released my shoulder.

I stared at him and felt my jaw lock. I didn't want him to come. Asking him to take this risk because of me was unfathomable. But, I recognized that look in his eye. It was the same utterly determined gaze that I knew well. It was clear that it didn't matter what I said, Eric would do what he thought was right. There was no stopping him. I just hoped I was getting saintly Eric, and not evil Eric. There was no way to know.

I folded my arms and said, "Fine. Show me how to open it."

"Not so fast," he said, blocking the fresco. "The living can't enter the Underworld. Both of us are alive. You need to seal yourself so the demons can't sense you. And so the Guardian can't tell you're alive. They need to think you're a Valefar. They need to think that both of us are Valefar."

"Damn it," I pushed my hair out of my face, annoyed that I'd already forgotten things Al had told me. "I forgot about the Guardian. Al said it would be the worst thing I could imagine." I paused wondering what that would be. The worst thing I could imagine wasn't possible. It already happened. Apryl already died. Collin was already in Hell. "I don't know what the Guardian will be." Uncertainty plagued my stomach, but I had no choice but to go forward. I had to take this path. There was no going backwards. "I know how to trick them into thinking we're Valefar—both of us."

I concentrated, and pressed my finger against the ruby in my ring. Shadows slinked from their hiding places in the cracks and crevices of the tomb. The cold fingers of shadows stroked my skin making me shiver. They were impossibly cold. I pulled as many shadows as I could tolerate. They coated my skin as they traveled down my throat and pooled in my stomach. The shadows would shroud me, locking in my scent, as long as I held them in place. They reeked of death and decay. That fragrance would mask my scent well enough. I'd have to get used to the discomfort of their corpse-like coldness inside of me. As for Eric, he was a pure Martis. His blood smelled like a Christmas buffet. I had to mask it with something stronger. Shadows alone wouldn't work.

Looking around the ancient tomb, I what I needed and decided to do it. There were no other options. Surely the deceased wouldn't mind. I walked to a pile of bones stacked neatly to the ceiling, and squatted down. I pressed my fingers into the dirt looking for something that would work—something that would be small enough.

I needed a shard, a single small piece of human bone. The bones of the dead would amplify the shadow's ability to conceal Eric's scent. It would smell of someone long deceased. I honestly didn't know what I was doing, or if it would even work. But, it had to work. Something inside me told me that it would. But, I needed something to bind the shadow to the bone, too. What was powerful enough to do that? And it had to be something within my reach. *Just find the bone, Ivy.* I thought to myself. *Figure out the rest later.* My fingers pressed against something smooth and hard. I dug it out of the earth. Eric asked what I was doing. I ignored him, and continued to dig it out. The bone shard was the size of my pinkie, and perfectly smooth. I cracked it in half and threw the other piece on the ground.

Turning to Eric I held up the bone and said, "You'll have to wear this around your neck." He looked at me oddly for a moment, and then nodded.

Now the hard part. I had to infuse the bone with shadow and keep it there. I focused and called the shadows to me, and when they responded I redirected them into the bone. I felt the shard turn icy cold in my hand. It worked! But, when I stopped focusing and trying to control them, the shadows spilled out. A bone wasn't a shadow container. It wasn't enough. There was nothing to hold them in place. What kept the shadows inside of me from spilling out?

Nothing.

They just stayed because I told them to. I looked at the bone. Talking to it wasn't going to do anything. No, that had to be only part of it. The shadows came because I called them. But why did they stay? What held them inside of me? I rubbed my finger along the sharp edge of the bone. It was a nervous habit. I fidgeted when I was tense. And it was a good thing too. By accident, a spike on the shard snagged my pinky and opened up a bright red wound. Blood seeped out and the bone soaked it up like a sponge. I looked at the bone, still white, but the tiny drop of blood was gone.

Acting on instinct, I pressed my finger hard across the jagged edge of bone. The flesh tore open and a scarlet drop of blood appeared on my fingertip. The bone was old and porous. Its tiny holes absorbed the blood flowing from my finger like a dry quill soaking up ink. Eric and I both knew that the substance that flowed through my veins was nearly entirely demon blood, with very little Martis left. Demon blood was powerful. That must be what commands the shadows and contains them. It's not my mind that controls the shadows—it's my blood.

When I was done, I swallowed hard wondering if Eric would take it. He detested demon blood. I handed the bone amulet to Eric wondering what he would do. I also wondered what it meant if he took it. "It has to touch your skin or it won't work."

Eric took the bone, nodding. He attached it to one of the woven necklaces he always wore. I expected him to say something, but he didn't. He quietly threaded the bone and hung it around his neck. Then he hid it under his shirt against his chest.

When he looked up, he asked, "Are you wearing Apryl's necklace?"

I nodded, as my hand reached for the necklace. Feeling the pendant beneath my fingers reassured me in a way I didn't understand. The ivory peonies were rough against my fingers while the brimstone disc was smooth against my thumb. I never took it off. My sister had sent it back with my Celestial Silver comb last year before she died. It was the last piece of her that I had. It was stupid, but when I wore that necklace, I felt like she was there with me.

But, why did Eric want it? What would Apryl's necklace do? Understanding flashed across my face. I smiled and said, "It opens the portal, doesn't it? The same way it did the night the Valefar used it to open the portal on Long Island? It's a key." He nodded. Apryl had a key to the Underworld. I sighed, not understanding why she had it or the comb. "I wish I'd gotten my comb back. I can't stand that they have it."

Eric ran his fingers along the wall slowly until they sunk into a small round depression next to the fresco with the the Valefar mark. "They don't have it. I do," Eric turned, reaching into his pocket, and withdrew a silver gleaming comb with a purple butterfly set in stones.

I threw my arms around him before taking it out of his hands. He smiled at me and then turned back to the wall.

I squealed, "Oh my God! Thank you! How'd you get it? They took it from me. I thought I'd never see it again." I couldn't wipe the shocked smile off my face.

"Yeah, well, let's just say a Martis shouldn't be without celestial silver. And no one bothered to search me. I knew if things went badly that they would take mine away. And they did. I had to make sure we had something—and yours was easy to take. So I took it."

"Eric! You stole it?" I asked, completely shocked.

"No!" He looked offended. "It's yours. I was going to return it to you, should the time come. And it did." He removed his finger from the indentation in the wall. "Ivy, press the pendant on the necklace into this slot. Brimstone side facing out." He backed away from the wall and my Brimstone necklace.

"When did you know that the disc on my necklace was Brimstone?" He trusted me more than I thought. One flick, one tiny wound from my pendant, and he'd die.

"I was the Seeker, remember?" He pointed at my necklace and said, "The Kreturic Pendant and the Prophecy One would find each other. I didn't recognize it at first. It wasn't until I found out your mark was purple that I pieced it together. The pendant marks the Prophecy One."

I turned the pendant over in my palm. I'd seen a drawing of it in a book at Eric's house. Curiosity ignited within me and I wanted to ask him more, but decided now wasn't the time. I pressed the pendant into the wall. When the peonies touched the slot the ground began to shake. It felt like something enormous had slammed into the ground. The loose bones shook free from their places. Old plaster cracked on the walls and crashed to the floor. The wall next to the grave, which appeared to be another unmarked tomb, began to slide away. We both stood still, watching, as the wall slid back and revealed thick darkness on the other side.

I swallowed hard. "This is it. There's no going back." My breath was shallow, as my skin prickled with anxiety. I turned to Eric, "Are you sure?"

"Completely."

The sound of feet slamming into the ground kept us from walking through the portal. I spun around, with my comb extended towards the noise. The razor sharp tines extended. I knew who it was before I could see her. Shannon's long hair flashed burnt orange as I recognized her long stride. "They are coming!" she screamed. "Casey told them you were here! You have to leave. Leave now!"

She stopped, doubling over on her knees. Eric looked at her, and back at the portal. "Do they know you're here? Do they know you came to warn us?" She nodded her head. Eric turned to me, "Ivy, we can't leave her here. They'll kill her if they think she tried to help us."

Without another word I grabbed the other piece of bone shard from the dirt, filled it with shadows and sealed them in with my blood. The shard was ice cold.

I said to Shannon, "Hang this around your neck and pretend you're a Valefar. We were going through that portal. All of us." Her body tensed, but she didn't refuse. A noise echoed behind her and we all jumped at the sound.

Martis. Lots of them.

I took a deep breath, pulled Apryl's necklace out of the slot, and we stepped through the portal.

CHAPTER FOURTEEN

The grave slid closed behind us, and drowned out the sounds of the approaching mob of Martis. I hesitated before taking a step forward. We were in the Underworld; the world of the dead and the damned. The Martis would not follow us here. To do so risked everything. No, they would stay in the catacombs waiting for us to return. Now we had other things to worry about.

I breathed in the cool air, and looked around. I don't know what I expected, but it was kind of lackluster in there. We were standing in a cavern. It stretched higher than the eye could see, and there was a single path carved into the stone in front of us. House-sized, pointed stalagmites would keep any adventurous folks from wandering off the path. The sounds of water dripping surrounded us, but the path was dry. Cawing birds echoed somewhere in the distance. The sound was eerie. I swallowed hard and looked back at Eric and Shannon.

"This is it," I said. My heart was racing. It felt like I was just doused with a bucket of dread. Shannon's eyes widened as her mouth fell opened. Eric's face held a similar expression. I turned slowly, knowing that the Guardian was standing behind me. Thoughts rushed at me as my mind tried to prepare for what it would see. But, there was no amount of preparation that would have made the Guardian less horrifying. Clutching my comb in my hand, I turned, thinking that the Guardian would be a beast. I expected that we would have to kill it to pass into the Underworld, and we had to pass. The lub-dub of my heart was so loud I thought everyone could hear it. As my eyes landed on the Guardian—I froze. Suddenly I couldn't breathe, I couldn't think.

She looked exactly the same. Her voice was laced with the rich tones that I remembered, "You cannot enter here. Turn back and return to where you came from." She held a brimstone sword and blocked our path with her body.

I stood there dumbly, too shocked to respond. Too shocked to do anything but feel my shattered heart tearing in half again. She repeated herself, but I couldn't move. I couldn't believe what I was seeing. My breath caught in my throat, as my hand flew to my mouth. She looked exactly the way I remembered her; long flowing hair the color of the setting sun, wide curious eyes that were never quite sure if they preferred blue or green, and the same pale sweetheart-shaped face that I had. Everything was the same with one glaring difference—a red scar marred her perfect complexion above her brow.

I choked out her name, "Apryl?"

My emotions were strangling me. It couldn't be her. No. No! My hands flew to my hair as I shook my head, taking a step away from her. Eric's hand was on my shoulder pulling me back. Shannon stood silently staring, too shocked to move. I sucked in a strangled gasp of air still unwilling to believe what was in front of me.

My sister was a Valefar.

Her eyes narrowed, "How do you know my name?" She pointed the blade at us, looking at us more closely now. No recognition flashed across her face when she saw me. She didn't know me. But, when her gaze fell on Eric she visibly bristled.

Her voice turned dark and menacing, "You...You're the one who did this to me!" Her eyes burned with hatred. "You were there the day I died. I'll never forget your face." She lifted her blade towards Eric. "Don't deny it. The only thing I remember about my previous life is how I died. Every grizzly detail is etched in my mind. I can see it when I close my eyes, when I try to remember who I was, and what happened to me. And you were there! You led them to me." She took a step closer to him, ignoring Shannon and I. "Do you know what they did to me? Did you stay around to watch?"

I swallowed hard, forcing my neck to turn towards Eric. I couldn't shake my shock. She remembered Eric, but not me? It felt like someone was choking me. I couldn't stand it. She was Valefar. She was the Guardian I'd have to kill to pass into the Underworld.

But Apryl was still fuming at Eric. She was singularly fixated on him. Rage filled her eyes with venom that I've never seen before.

A chill racked me violently and I couldn't stop shaking. "What's she talking about?" I asked Eric. "You led the Valefar to her? And then you watched her die?" Horror choked me so that I could barely utter the words. He didn't. That would be hideously cruel. Dear God, please deny it Eric.

Apryl's eyes burned with anger. "Tell her," Apryl commanded, "Yes, let's tell her. But I think this story should come from me." Apryl's eyes were narrowed into thin slits. She gazed at me intently for a few moments without speaking. Her head tilted to the side, and her expression softened. "I know you," she said uncertainly to me. "I can't remember why or where, but I know you. Don't I?" I nodded, unable to speak to her. I was muted by fear and grief. She waited for me to say where she knew me from, but I couldn't answer.

Having this conversation wasn't something I ever imagined. Valefar don't remember their previous lives, except for how they died. That they remember in vivid detail. It's a way to inflict pain on the new Valefar and allow them to carry that pain for the rest of their immortal lives. She remembered Eric because he was there, but she didn't remember me. She didn't remember her sister because I wasn't there. And I couldn't find the strength within me to tell her.

She finally said, "Well, it doesn't matter now anyway. It doesn't matter how hard I try, I won't ever remember you. And from the shocked expression on your face, I'm guessing you thought I was dead. Death would have been better than what happened to me.

"About a year ago I sat alone on a dock in Italy. My friend and I had been laughing and enjoying the sunshine. She ran off to get gelato, and I decided to swing my legs off the end of the pier and wait for her. I heard footfalls behind me. I was surprised she returned so quickly, but when I turned it wasn't her standing behind me—it was him." She gestured to Eric. "I remember those golden eyes staring at me, drinking me in. It made my pulse race and I blushed. I actually blushed! No one had ever looked at me like that before. I smiled at him, but he said nothing. He just stared. I got to my feet, and walked over to him, barefoot in my little sundress. I thought something was wrong… like he was lost or something. I thought I could help. But, before I reached him, he turned abruptly, and walked away. He disappeared into the crowded street and I didn't see him again. I thought nothing of it at the time. Maybe he was lost. Maybe he thought I was someone else. There had to be some reason for his strange behavior. And there was.

"I settled back at the end of the dock, and hung my legs over the side. When I looked up, I saw him standing on the opposite pier. That was the last time I saw daylight. Someone rushed at me, and pulled me over the edge. I screamed as we fell into the water. I tried to swim to the surface, but they wouldn't let me." She took a steadying breath before continuing. "We were underwater. He yanked my hair away from my face, pushing it off of my forehead. I couldn't breathe. He stared as if he couldn't believe that nothing was there. Then his lips smashed down on mine. Violently, he kissed me with his arms crushing me to him. He held me like that until every last bit of soul was ripped from my dying body. When he pulled me to the surface, I didn't gasp for breath. I couldn't do anything.

"His words echoed around me as he spoke to someone else. The other voices were uncertain. They kept asking, *Is she the one?* But, they didn't know. So, one of them took a blade and cut a gash in my head right here," she pointed to her scar, "and another slit his finger and rubbed his blood into the wound. They laughed while they did it, passing me around like a rag doll. They all kissed me, but there was no soul left to take. After a while, they took more than kisses. They touched me. They used my body however they wanted. When they were done, I thought I'd climb onto the shore and cry. I thought someone would find me. But they didn't give me the chance. The boy who knocked me into the water took out a silver blade no bigger than my finger. It was wrapped in fine cloth, like it was some precious metal. He jabbed its sharp edge into my stomach and twisted. I screamed out in pain, but no one heard me. No one saw. Except him. When the Valefar dropped me into the water, I slid beneath the surface and through a portal. I've been here ever since."

Eric had remained silent until then, and said, "And Kreturus saw you? And posted you here?"

Apryl's jaw locked as she spit out the words, "Yes, that demon owns me now because of you! They told him that I was someone else, and his disappointment was brutal when he found out that I wasn't." She stared at Eric with hatred in her eyes. "It was you. Your fault. You led them to me."

Eric didn't look away; he didn't waiver, "It was my fault."

"Then I think you should die a death ten times more painful, and more humiliating than what I went through." Her face contorted as she filled with rage. The black sword swung in an arch towards Eric. It collided with the blades of my silver weapon, as I stepped between her and Eric.

"You can't kill him," I said. "He's already dead, and he was told to bring me this way." I strained pushing back against her blade. "Lower your weapon."

Apryl let out a hysterical laugh. "Lower my weapon? No one can pass this way no matter what you say. And since you didn't turn to leave, you'll die too." She lifted her blade and swung it at me. I blocked her again, not wanting to advance. I couldn't hurt her. It didn't matter that she didn't know me anymore. I was still thrilled to see her—thrilled and terrified.

I took a step back, disconnecting our blades, "I won't fight you, but you have to let us pass."

She laughed again, but it was hollow. "Let you pass? This isn't the way into some park. It's a road to certain destruction." She stepped towards me, swinging her blade again. We were backed up against the cavern wall. "Last chance Little Princess. Turn back."

As the words fell out of her mouth, all the fight drained from her body. She called me Little Princess when we fought at home. Mom would tell her to be nice, but that was her go to name when I got what I wanted and she didn't. Did she remember me? Her eyes widened as she looked at my face. Her blade fell limply at her side. The memory was inside of her, but out of reach. She didn't remember me. When she spoke again, I knew she didn't. "All three of you want to pass this way, but none of you will want to pay the price. You might as well turn back."

Shannon spoke, "Why don't you let us decide that. What's the price?"

Apryl's eyes slid between Shannon, Eric, and me. "What kind of Valefar are you? How do you not know that!" She laughed at us for a second, then her expression changed and the laughter died in her mouth. "Oh my God! You aren't Valefar, are you? Otherwise you'd know the price. You'd also know that there is no way you could pay it." She inhaled deeply, and a slight smile crept across her face. I recognized that smile. It was conjured from the delight in smelling mortal blood, and Martis blood was even more potent. She was trying to catch our scent.

I spoke before anyone else could, "I'm damned. It doesn't matter what I am. Or what I'm not. I was sent here. Kreturus wants me and this is the entrance I chose. Tell me the price. I'm passing this way no matter what it cost."

She slid her fingers along the edge of her black blade, and tilted her head back. "Well, good luck with that. Only the living can pass this way. They must cast their spirit into the Pool of Lost Souls. Admission here isn't cheap. It isn't some amusement park filled with cheap thrills. The damned are enslaved here for eternity. Do you really want to cast off your soul? Or whatever you have? I'm still wondering why I can't catch your scent." She sniffed at me, looking perplexed.

"Never mind that," I said. "The Pool of Lost Souls, what is it? How do we do it and does it require a soul for passage or just a piece of a soul?"

A smile slid across her face, "So, you've dealt with Valefar before, huh? The Pool of Lost Souls is what binds your body to the Underworld. Once it contains your soul, you belong to Kreturus. But you're right. It doesn't require an entire soul for passage. If you can bear the agony, it will take a severed soul and allow you to pass."

I turned to Eric and Shannon. "It's a Demon Kiss, isn't it?"

Eric nodded, "That's what it sounds like. And there is no way around it. The Underworld entrances require payment. I just had no idea what it was. If you want to keep going, you don't even have to ask me, Ivy. I'm coming."

I turned to Shannon, "You should go back and hide. They won't find you. And besides, it's me and Eric that they really want. I can't ask you to come with me."

Her green eyes were serious for once, "Who said you had to ask? Ivy, I'll pay the price. I'm not letting you go down there alone."

Turning back to Apryl, I reluctantly looked her in the eye. She didn't remember me. I couldn't touch her. I couldn't hug her and tell her everything would be all right. For all I knew, it wouldn't. Suppressing the thoughts, I said, "Take us to the Pool of Lost Souls." I never thought I'd volunteer for a Demon Kiss, but as it turned out, that wasn't exactly what it was.

CHAPTER FIFTEEN

I followed my sister relieved that I didn't have to fight her. That was one thing that I wouldn't have been able to do. Shannon and Eric remained silent as we walked. Panicked thoughts brushed my mind. I had no idea if I could bear another demon kiss, or if my soul would survive the encounter. I'd already been attacked by a Valefar a few months ago, and lost all but a small piece of my soul. And that piece I severed willingly to bring Collin back to life. I was playing a deadly game and I knew it. At some point, the amount of spirit left in my body would not be enough to sustain the angel blood that flowed through my veins. When that time came, the demon blood would overtake me, and I'd become a full-fledged Valefar.

My nails bit into my palms, making me realize exactly how much that scared me. Being enslaved was the worst thing I could possibly imagine. As weeks slid into months, I had started to see that my fate was simply foretold. The only person to blame for casting that dark destiny in stone was me. It was completely my fault. It was my fault because I couldn't abandon Collin, and I couldn't watch a sword slice Eric in two. And now, I couldn't deny the price of passage into the Underworld, even though it was more than I could pay.

We followed Apryl along the cavern pathways. The stone glowed a faint reddish brown like it was illuminated from within. Water was forever dripping from somewhere, but I never saw the source. Periodically the sound of beating wings filled the air, but I never saw what made that noise either. The Underworld wasn't like anything I'd expected.

A chill ran through me when I first saw the Caribbean blue waters. They looked so out of place, lapping at the jagged dark stone that stretched from floor to higher than the eye could see. The light blue water stood out against the dismal backdrop like an oasis of hope in the midst of despair. Its false promise of peace was part of what made the Pool of Lost Souls so deadly. The second part I would soon learn.

Eric, Shannon, and I stopped a few feet from the water's edge. As I watched the crystal blue liquid move, I realized it wasn't made of water at all. Instead it was thick like gel, swirling and lapping at the shore. Streaks of pale green, laced with sea foam, swirled suspended in its depths. The Pool stretched on forever, and despite the crystal clarity, the bottom was not visible. I swallowed hard, not liking this mutant-water one bit.

"Step to the water's edge, but do not step into the Pool. If you do, the lost souls will pull you in. Your feet must stay on dry ground," Apryl warned.

I looked at her, and asked, "Why are you helping us? Aren't you the Guardian?"

She looked at me with that expression of hers. The one that said she liked you, but she thought you were a total idiot. It was a glimpse of the old Apryl. "I'm helping you because…" she shrugged, "I'm not sure. It's like I know you or something."

Shannon's green eyes were wide as she looked from me back to the Pool. "It's going to be deceptive, isn't it?" She swallowed hard. "There is no way to just cast some soul in and walk away, is there?"

Apryl didn't answer. Instead she turned her dark eyes to me and said, "Nothing down here is as it seems. Don't embrace the waters or anything that comes from them." Embrace the waters? I had no idea what she meant, but nodded at her anyway. It dawned on me that she may not be helping us, as I'd thought. She wasn't my sister anymore. She was a Valefar. I wondered if I should believe her, but why would she lie? I'd already volunteered for a demon kiss. How much worse could it be? As I looked harder at the Pool, I could see the green streaks moving more rhythmically, as if they were waiting for us to join in and dance. "Step to the edge and do what you must." Apryl extended her arm, and stepped away from us.

Swallowing hard, I turned toward Eric and then Shannon, "Ready?" The nodded in unison. My chest felt like it was going to tear open as I took those few short steps. The blue swirled in thick slow circles, as the pale green shapes rose and fell below the surface. As I got closer, I saw that the shapes were people. Their forms swam in the Pool, suspended, and trapped for eternity. Eyes wide, I turned in panic to look at Eric. I had no idea there were people in there, but he didn't see me.

His face paled as his eyes widened, fixated on the Pool in front of him. His body was shaking as he stood staring transfixed on her face. A whisper of a word slid out of his throat, "Lydia."

The terror in his eyes made me turn back to the water. I didn't understand what was happening until I turned. A familiar face strode towards me across the Pool's surface. His skin glowed with a pale shimmer, but his eyes were still sapphire blue. My chest heaved as a sharp pain tore through me, stealing my breath. Collin. It was Collin walking towards me. I was no longer aware of the others. My only thoughts were of Collin—the scent of his skin, the feel of his touch on my cheek, the taste of his lips on mine.

My foot lifted to take a step towards him when a voice snapped me back to reality, "Stay where you are little sister, or you'll never survive." Apryl's voice made my neck snap towards her. She held my gaze and repeated the warning. "It's not really him. This creature has come to take your soul. It'll pull you into the Pool if you let it."

My voice caught in my throat as I looked back at him. I was mesmerized. It didn't even dawn on me until later that she said, *little sister*. She remembered me, but I was so transfixed on Collin walking towards me that I didn't notice. "No, it can't be true. That's him. It's the good part that was stolen. He wouldn't hurt me. I know it." Reassurance flooded my body every time I looked at the figure on the water. I hadn't seen him since the night he saved me. And now he was right in front of me, only steps away. If I just stepped closer, I could wrap my arms around him again.

"It's not him. That's the Guardian. It's pulled every single person who tried to pass into this Pool. I can't stop you from trying to pass it. I'm bound to the Pool. I can't go past this point. But, you can if you remember that this isn't who you think it is. If you remember not to touch it and pay passage." She folded her arms and leaned back against the cave wall.

I turned back to the water's edge. My breath caught in my throat as Collin's form stood right in front of me with his ankles submerged in the lapping waters. I wanted to throw my arms around him and feel his warm body against mine, but I hesitated. Looking into his eyes, I waited for him to speak, but he said nothing. His face slowly showcased my favorite expressions— the one that made it impossible to deny him anything.

Apryl's voice broke the silence, "Ivy, I'm in there too." Shocked, I turned to look at her. Sadness weighed on her soft features, deeply carving lines into her face that hadn't been there before. "I've stood on the water's edge seeing the one thing that I desire most, but cannot have—myself. I watch her come to the edge, but I'm unable to do anything about it. She's like an image trapped in a reflection. There is no way to undo what was done to me. Or him. Only the ruler of the Underworld has that power." Apryl's words sunk into me. She'd tried to get her soul back. She'd stood here and been unable to reclaim her life, even though it was right in front of her. I closed my eyes hard, and looked away. Demons were cruel. They never let you forget your place, and every action was doused with pain.

Just then Eric snapped. His foot lifted forward and then the other.

"No!" I screamed, but it was too late. He had stepped into the crystal blue liquid. The waters surrounded the single foot that touched the water, as Eric cried out in pain.

His scream awoke Shannon from her dazed trance, no doubt seeing someone she loved manifested in front of her. Someone she wanted, but couldn't have. She shook her head and ran toward Eric, careful not to touch the water. "What do we do?" she asked as she went to pull him back.

"No! Don't touch him! It might be able to pull you in too!" Panic was flooding me. Eric's back arched as he let out a raw scream, frozen by the waters that trapped him. His face contorted with pain as his body shook.

I recognized that scream. It was the sound Martis made when they were being demon kissed. The Guardian was sucking his soul into the Pool. There was no time. If I waited another second we would lose him. I wasn't certain if we could touch him or not, but there was no other choice. I threw myself between the Guardian and Eric. Lydia's pale likeness melted down into the water and Collin was the only figure remaining. His blue eyes pierced me, making me think I couldn't possibly do this, but there was no other choice.

Reaching behind me, I touched my fingertips to Eric's chest. A pulsing pale purple light came from my fingers and sent a shock through him. I pushed him back onto the shore, where he collapsed. It was completely silent. My heart thundered in my chest as I strode further into the lake and up to Collin's form. With each step I took forward, he took one back. But I kept walking towards him. The thing was, with each passing step, it looked more and more like him. I kept telling myself, *This isn't him. It's not him.* But, his eyes made me doubt myself. These waters made me uncertain. They held power that I didn't understand and made me question everything I knew. If I was closer to Collin, I could tell if it was truly him.

Contact with the Pool didn't make me writhe as I stepped into the waters. I felt the cold snares trying to snake through my legs, searching for my soul, but I had very little soul left to steal. I hoped they wouldn't find it before I reached the Guardian—the perfect image of Collin. My pulse pumped the blood through my body so fast that it felt like I'd run miles. Anticipation and dread pooled together violently in my stomach as I neared him. His cool eyes rested on me, watching me approach. He ignored Shannon, as she dragged Eric out of sight.

Apryl sat watching, eyes wide and mouth hanging open.

This is an illusion, I told myself. *It's not him.* Certainty washed over me as he stood inches from my body. I could reach out and touch him. So, I did. I threw my arms around his neck and pressed my lips against his. A cold blast was created as soon as our lips joined. It collided with the shadows I called to shroud my scent. Combined, they tore through me in a wave of sharp, cold pain. The familiar feeling of flesh ripping from bone consumed me. As the piece of soul I had remaining, broke free, I shivered. If he took that piece, if it was large enough, I would be Valefar. And yet, this was the only way to pass into the Underworld without Kreturus being aware of my presence. I felt the golden warmth of my spirit traveling rapidly towards my lips. I hoped I knew what I was doing. There was nothing to base my decision on, but a hunch. When my soul passed my heart, the coldness clamped down harder. It felt like I was being crushed under a massive block of ice. My body was resisting, but I could feel it wouldn't be mine to command much longer if I finished this kiss. The Pool was already doing something to me. I felt the demon blood coursing through my veins like shards of glass. I wanted to scream out unable to endure the pain.

My soul approached my mouth slowly, like it was caught on a line. The Guardian's kiss carefully pulled it closer and closer to my lips. His fingers threaded through my hair, gently brushing my cheek. It was the way Collin had kissed me. That kiss lingered in my thoughts constantly. I leaned into him wishing it were Collin. My eyelids suddenly became heavy, as a flash of warmth shot through my belly. The pain was erased. It made me feel like I could stay like this forever with him—just the two of us, wrapped together, with his lips on mine. When I leaned into him more, a distant voice shrieked, but I didn't stop. This was where I wanted to be. This is where I was safe. Here with Collin. Bliss shot through me, coursing through my veins and making me feel invincible.

It wasn't until I felt the warmth of my soul flood my mouth, that I heard his voice.

A faint voice brushed the inside of my mind. *It's not me Ivy. Drive the Guardian back before there is nothing left of you.*

Collin? Collin! I could hear him! Oh God, then who was I kissing? Fear snapped me back to reality. Before I knew what overtook me, my powers surged. Black mist swirled around me, encasing my soul-ravaged body. A bright light no larger than a spec of sand flashed. At the same time, I was thrown back onto the shore. The remaining piece of my soul slid back down my throat when I hit the ground, and warmed my blood in the process. Disoriented, I looked over at the lake to see Collin's ethereal form shoot back into the Pool and dissolve into the waters. I breathed deeply, relieved.

But, this wasn't over yet. The creature resurfaced, snarling with a mouth filled of daggers. Its water-like form was blazing with blue and green flames. The Guardian's red eyes locked with mine as it cried out in rage. Too terrified to move, I stood there watching. The Guardian shot across the water, making a deafening noise that paralyzed me with terror. My heart was about to explode in my chest. There wasn't enough air to fill my heaving lungs.

A hand pulled at my shoulder urgently, "Go! Go now! Once you pass, it can't touch you." Apryl was yelling in my face, but I couldn't move. She slammed her body into mine, attempting to force my legs forward. "Ivy! Move! It can still reach you! Move now or die!" But her words rolled off of me. I couldn't move. It didn't matter that I knew I would die if I stayed here. It was like I was trapped by something I couldn't see. The Guardian was somehow holding me in place. Before I knew what was happening, the Guardian was in front of me. Its shining silver teeth gleamed red in the glow of the cave making them look like they were covered in blood. It let out another ear piercing cry, and lunged at me.

Every muscle in my body heaved, trying to move before those teeth ripped the flesh from my bones. But it didn't matter how hard my muscles flinched or how fast my heart pumped, I was trapped. A scream erupted from my throat right before the creature's teeth ripped into me. My arms flew up to cover my face when another scream drew my attention back to the Guardian. The piercing cry tore through the power that immobilized me.

It was Apryl's voice—Apryl's cry. She'd thrown herself between me and the Guardian still screaming at me to run. When I didn't move, she'd stepped in front of me allowing the razor sharp teeth to tear through her arm. Three deep red gashes slashed through her pale skin from shoulder to wrist. She cradled the bleeding arm close to her body, screaming in agony. The creature lunged for her again, teeth first. I watched in horror. This couldn't be happening. I just found her. And now this beast had me trapped and it was ripping my sister's skin from her body.

The Guardian's teeth sank into her other arm, jerking her away from me with a flick of its head. The creature was twice my height. Its mouth was covered in my sister's blood. Her voice no longer filled the cavern with screams. Rage seared through me. The Guardian did not release the bonds that immobilized me, but my powers were greater. Heat burned through me, but I had no idea how the power would manifest itself. A raw screamed ripped out of my throat, as the Guardian's bloody red teeth rushed at my face. When its sharp edges clamped down to bite into my flesh a loud crack erupted, and the teeth that touch my skin exploded. Silver blood-covered shards flew through the air, as the creature screamed in horror. It lunged at me again, but the same thing happened. When the silver teeth touched my skin there was a loud crack and more of its teeth shattered. Sweat covered my cowering body.

The beast's cry filled the cavern, as it became increasingly enraged. Its eyes flamed red, as it lunged at me one last time. It lifted its maw directly above me. Saliva dripped off the remaining silver dagger-like teeth, dripping onto my body below. Terror coursed through my veins. The Guardian changed the way it would attack. Its wide spread jaws were going to swallow me whole. It shrieked as its massive head lunged toward me. The thick scaly maw snatched me from where I stood.

As soon as the Guardian's lips closed around me, everything went dark. The bonds that had immobilized me below were now broken. I could move. The creature's tongue was trying to push me towards the back of its mouth. It swept at me, trying to knock me over and shove me down its throat. A dull violet glow filled the creature's mouth. My hair was still flaming. That meant that I still had the power I'd conjured before. The Guardian's tongue swept past me once as I fell between its tongue and its teeth. I extended my arms and quickly grabbed hold of a tooth, and hoped that it would still work. Burying my face in my shoulder, I looked away as the loud crack echoed in its mouth. When its tooth shattered, the Guardian's maw opened in a raw scream.

As soon as its jaws shot opened, I jumped. It was impossibly high, but it was better than being eaten. But,

I wasn't out of harm's way yet. As I fell to the ground, it snapped at me, trying to catch me. The Guardian was moderately successful. I fell on the outside of his maw. My hand collided with its massive red eye. The Guardian shook violently, but I lodged my fingers in its eyelid and had no plans to let go. The power was still in my hands. I could feel it coursing through to my fingertips. I held onto the Guardian's eyelid with one hand and sunk my other five fingers straight into its flame red eye. The crack erupted, echoing off the cave walls, as the Guardian's eye exploded in its socket. Its head shook violently as it bellowed, but I held on.

Did I have to kill this thing to pass the Pool of Lost Souls? Or could I sneak by? I wasn't certain. I also had no idea why my hands were making things explode. Was that coming from me? Or was it like putting gunpowder next to a campfire? Some things just ignited each other. I wasn't sure, but it knew it was now or never. I pulled the silver comb from my hair and touched it to my mark extending the tines into long razor sharp blades. Creatures of darkness could only be killed with Celestial Silver. It was possible the beast would shake its head and I'd fall while I reached for my comb, but I had to. Something told me that blowing up both eyes wouldn't work. I had to sink my blade into the beast. Without another thought, I lunged at the Guardian's other eye. The blade sank deep into its pupil in one swift stroke. The Guardian cried out, shaking its head. My body was thrown to the ground. I was right in front of it. If it wanted me, it could have lunged again and it would have my soul. All of it. But the Guardian turned its blind head from me and slid back below the surface of the water.

An eerie silence drifted over the Pool. Shannon and Eric were nowhere in sight. Neither was Apryl. I slowly stood, although every bone in my body protested. Something glimmered to my right. I bent to pick it up. It was a shard of the Guardian's silver tooth. It was thin and jagged where the tooth cracked. I wiped the blood and flesh from the point, and tied it to my belt out of sight. I might need it. My heart was still racing when Apryl walked up behind me.

"You beat the shit out of the Guardian." Apryl sounded amused.

I turned to look at her, not expecting what I saw. Valefar were supposed to heal quickly from non-fatal wounds. Especially if no silver was used. Her arms were both marred. The fleshed peeled away from bone in places. Her face was white. "Apryl...Oh my God. Why aren't you healing?"

She collapsed next to me. "It'll heal. Eventually. His teeth were celestial silver filled with sapphire serum. Every single tooth. The Martis originally put the Guardian here. The Guardian kept the living out and kept the demons in. The sapphire serum makes it more deadly. Damn Martis. Basically, if it buries its teeth deep enough in you, you're dead no matter what. It doesn't matter if you're Martis or Valefar, demon or angel. That stuff is deadly no matter what you are. The Guardian's sapphire serum rips the soul from the living, and its razor sharp tooth tears the flesh from the dead. No one gets past that thing, but you shattered its teeth and blinded it." She let out a weak laugh. "You're insane."

"Will it heal?" I asked looking back at the water.

"Doubt it. Nothing is more deadly than Celestial Silver to Underworld creatures. It seems to amplify wounds, and prevents them from healing. I've seen Valefar try to get the thing to back off with brimstone weapons, but the Guardian just snapped them like twigs. It's something about the teeth being infused with the sapphire serum and being made of Celestial Silver. It's stronger…More powerful. That combined with whatever you did—well, it won't heal. But I doubt it'll die. That's what made me remember you." She smiled faintly.

"What do you mean?" I was glad she remembered me, but I didn't want to ask how. Was it because she sensed the demon blood flowing through my veins? Maybe she only recognized me as another Valefar.

"I can only remember things from the time of my death and forward. When I first saw Eric on the pier, I thought he looked like the kind of boy you'd date. You always went for the wholesome, nice-guy types." She was right. I did go for guys like Eric before she died. But that was a long time ago, before my life came crashing down around me. When she spoke again, her voice changed. It sounded distant and lost. "That's why I remembered. I watched you march up to that beast like you owned it when it attacked Eric. You protected him…against something that should have killed you. Only one person I ever knew was that crazy." She smirked, "My whack-job little sister. Who else would be crazy enough to show up down here? Everyone else wants to get out and you're trying to break in. God, I miss you…" She closed her teary eyes, as her head swayed.

"Whoa, Apryl." I rushed to her and held her upright. "What can I do?"

She went limp in my arms as I lowered her to the ground. Her eyes opened into little slits. "Kill the bastard responsible for making me into this thing. I'm not alive, but I'm not dead. I'd rather die, Ivy. If that thing—the Guardian—ripped me to pieces, it would have been worth it. I would have finally been free from this curse. But Kreturus made sure the Guardian wouldn't kill me. He did something to me so that the Guardian will only chomp on me once or twice before deciding I'm not worth eating."

"What curse? What are you talking about?" I kneeled next to her. Some of the color was returning to her face. Although her wounds still looked like raw meat.

"We're cursed, you and I. It's the curse of the Valefar. Some say we're damned, but it's not the same thing. Damned means you did something wrong before. It means you had a choice about what became of you." She shook her head softly, "But that isn't what happened. The curse of the Valefar is something that happens to you—whether you're good or bad. You have no choice, but to become this vile, soulless thing that doesn't deserve to be alive." Her expression was vacant as she spoke. "The demon blood gave me power to do and take whatever I wanted, except for the one thing I want more than anything. My soul. The curse leaves the person a shell of themselves. I can't remember much about my previous life, except that I loved it. The curse allowed me to remember some of my previous thoughts, enough to know that what I am is evil. Guilt gnaws at me, but I can't do a thing about it. I need souls to survive. I've killed people, Ivy. People who stumbled on the Pool. It doesn't happen often, but

I didn't let them get to the Pool. I'm evil. I'm one of the things that killed me on the pier. If I could kill myself, I would. That's why you have to kill him. Kill him for me, Ivy. Make him die in the same agony that I'm forced to live with for eternity."

The lump in my throat was so big that I couldn't swallow. The pain in her voice was unbearable. I'd do anything to make it better, but I was afraid to ask who she was talking about, even though I already knew. It could have been Eric, or the Valefar on the pier, but somehow I knew that wasn't who she meant. "Who, Apryl? Who are you talking about?"

Her hazel eyes pierced mine. She clutched my hands hard, and whispered his name with such utter hatred that I had no doubt she meant it. "Kreturus. Kill Kreturus." I nearly choked. She'd just asked me to do what the prophecy said I would do. Her words made my skin prickle. She saw the expression on my face. "That's what you're here for, isn't it?" She laughed hollowly, pulling her slashed arms tighter to her body. "There isn't one of us who hasn't wished that old demon was dead. And, I've never seen anyone do what you did to the Guardian. If you could do that, I bet you can kill him. There's something different about you. I can sense it. Kill him for me, Ivy. Kill him for stealing my life. Kill him for making me this monster. Kill him for taking me from you."

Those last words made my rage burn. Apryl's death was his fault. My mother's death, my house burning, the demon kiss, losing most of my soul, the pain, losing Collin—all of it was his fault. If Kreturus didn't want me so badly, none of those things would have happened. Apryl would be at home with Mom. The force that was destroying my life was his fault. I wanted to kill him at that moment. If it were possible, I would have buried my blade in his chest and did so with glee. But, I knew there would be major problems if I killed Kreturus. Somehow, if I killed him I would become Queen of the Underworld. I didn't know how that would happen, but it was part of the prophecy. I didn't want to stay down here. I didn't want to be the Demon Queen. Screw that! But, there was no point in explaining that now. There was no point at all. She was trapped here. The best I could do was to give her some hope. So I nodded at her, "I'll try. He has two things I want. And I'm not giving them up. Not for anything." I smiled at her, glad to talk to her again. Just sitting by her and hearing her voice was amazing. My sister was back from the dead. She was damaged, but she was still mine.

I stood up slowly. Apryl was sitting next to me, her arms slowly healing. "Come on. Let's go find Shannon and Eric. They have to be nearby. I'm glad they ran. There was no point in all three of us getting eaten, but I didn't see where they went. Hopefully, they didn't go too far." I brushed the dirt off of my jeans.

Apryl remained seated, leaning her head against a stone. "Can't. I'm bound to the Pool of Lost Souls. I can't leave here. I can move between the portal that you entered and the Pool. That's it."

I looked down at her for a moment. There was only one way to help her, and it was the same path that would free Collin. I'd have to kill Kreturus and deal with the consequences. "I'll come back for you."

She nodded up at me. "I hope so."

CHAPTER SIXTEEN

Leaving Apryl behind felt wrong, but I knew the Valefar could be forced to do certain things and they had to obey. She was bound to the Pool of Lost Souls and could not leave. My feet stumbled in the darkness. I could see all right, but I was so tired. I'd been walking for hours and was no closer to finding Eric and Shannon. It was difficult to keep track of time in this place. There was no natural rhythm to things; no rising or setting of the sun, no sleep or wake. I wasn't the only one down here who didn't sleep. The echoes of creatures could be heard constantly, never pausing, never falling into the natural silence of slumber.

I'd hoped to find Shannon and Eric by now, but it was becoming doubtful that I would see them again. Holding my arms tightly against my chest, I continued walking alone. They were down here somewhere, lost, because of me.

Eric's reaction at the Pool surprised me. I didn't expect him to be the one to falter and step into the Pool. If we hadn't been warned...   If we all walked into the Pool... I shook my head clearing the grizzly thought from my mind. It didn't matter now. They were gone. Lost. I'd be lucky if I ever saw them again. Hopefully they were still together.

Maybe the reason I hadn't seen them yet was that they turned back. It would have been easy to run from the Pool of Lost Souls and back out the portal. A small part of me hoped they turned back. It was possible that Shannon pulled Eric back to the entrance. Martis were strong. She could have dragged him the entire way. It was possible they were safe in the catacombs right now. But, if that were true then Eric wasn't safe. There was a crushing sensation in my chest as I thought about it. The Martis condemned him to death. Eric was in danger no matter where he went. I didn't know whether to grieve, because they were lost in the Underworld, or be upset that they ditched me and left. Or they could be dead—killed by some creature I'd yet to see. The thought of two people who cared about me dying before we even started was unbearable.

Don't think about it, I told myself. *They're fine. They're... somewhere else. Safe. Take care of Ivy. Keep walking. Don't stop.*

This place was too deadly to let fear overtake me. I had to focus. There were no more free passes, and no one left to help me. Having people with me had made me feel more secure. Even if we weren't best friends, we all wanted to stay alive. It gave us all a common goal, at least for a little while. There was no talk of demon blood, Seekers, or Martis. Now they were gone and a creepy feeling that I was being followed was gnawing at me. Ignoring it, I decided to focus on what I came here for—to get Collin out. I didn't even know how to find him down here.

After I passed the Pool of Lost Souls, the rocky terrain shifted to flatness. There was flat rock as far as I could see. It gave off the same dull rust-colored glow that was on most of the rocks here. Darkness masked the cavern ceiling. It was so high above me that creatures could fly overhead without me seeing them. I felt a gust of wind periodically or heard the flapping wings of some oversized creature. By the time I looked, they were either gone or masked by darkness that my Martis vision couldn't penetrate. The eerie sounds of dripping water and the calls of a million muffled birds echoed around me. The birds—at least I hoped they were birds—weren't next to me, but they were nearby.

There were so many paths to choose from that I had no idea which way to go. There was no trace of Eric and Shannon. I decided to keep heading towards Collin. If I met up with Shannon and Eric again, good. But if I didn't, I was here for Collin.

I took a step onto one of the paths, hesitated, and stepped back. Which way should I go? Where was he? I kicked at the dirt with my sneaker. Before I realized it, I was stepping onto each path. I stood there for a moment, moving the dirt around with my foot, and stepped back. The trails splintered into eight paths after the Pool. When I stepped on the second to last path, I felt something. I didn't expect it, but it was there. The bond. When I stood on that trail, the old feeling of the rubber band in my gut pulled me gently. It wanted me to go down this path. So, that was how I decided where to go. It took some time whenever I was at a junction, but I was sure I was going the right direction.

After walking for a while, I came to grips with the fact that I was alone. The odds of me finding Shannon and Eric again were miniscule. This place was a maze. And the deeper I went into the Underworld, the scarier it got. I wasn't sure how I was going to do this. I sat down hard, and leaned against a large rock that protruded from the ground. The cold crept through my torn tee shirt and felt good against my sore back. I closed my eyes for a moment. When I reopened them, Collin was standing in front of me.

His dark hair hung in his eyes, as he looked at me. At first I thought it was my imagination, or another demon trick to get me to fork over my soul. I drank him in anyway. God, I missed him so much. His voice. His smile. His touch. When he was around I felt more complete. More like the girl I should have been. I gazed at the Collin-mirage, wishing it were really him, but knowing that wasn't possible. He was a prisoner somewhere down here. His powers were gone, or he could have efanotated himself out. No, whatever stood in front of me was not Collin.

"Oh Ivy, you shouldn't have come here," he said. He didn't move towards me. He just stood there, looking down at me. My eyebrows rose on my face in disbelief. His voice. That was his voice. Could it be him? Was this really Collin? I rose slowly and took a step towards him. The bond tugged faintly. The bond. It's him! Without another thought, I rushed into his arms. He wrapped them tightly around me as I buried my face in his chest. Tears flowed down my cheeks, as I looked back up at him. His fingers laced through my hair. He looked at me like he thought he'd never see me again. He whispered, "You're not safe here. You need to go back."

I pulled away from him. "But, I came for you. And I found you. We can go back now. We can just leave this awful place." I threaded my fingers through his and pulled his warm hand, but he didn't move. He looked like he wanted to say something, but no words fell from his perfect lips. "What is it?" My eyes widened, as dread filled me. Something was wrong. Why wouldn't he tell me?

"I can't leave." He swallowed hard, with his blue eyes piercing mine.

I shook my head, not understanding. "What? Of course you can. I kicked the Guardian's ass. We can walk right past and he won't even see us leave. Collin, it's not far." But the expression on his face told me it had nothing to do with how far it was. I felt my heart sink into my stomach. "You have to tell me. I'm not leaving here without you. Tell me, Collin. Please."

He looked away from me, and pushed his hair away from his face. He squeezed his eyes shut and took a deep breath; "I'm not really here with you right now. I thought I felt the bond earlier and wanted to make sure you weren't here. I thought it might have been a vision, but it wasn't because here you are." He took my hands in his and spoke urgently. "You have to leave. The only reason I'm still alive is because I'm bait. They want you. They're keeping me hidden near Kreturus and hoping you'll come all the way down there to try and save me. You can't do this Ivy." He gently brushed my cheek.

"He wants you and will stop at nothing to get you. He wants your power. Please, promise me you won't do this. Please." His eyes were glassy as he begged me to turn back.

"I can't go back. No, please, listen to me. The Martis condemned me. If I go back to the surface they'll kill me. There is no safe place for me, Collin. There's nowhere to hide. I'm dead no matter where I go." I paused, pulling him to me. My fingers rested on his face, making him meet my eyes. "I can't leave you here. I love you, Collin. Don't tell me to turn back again. I can't do it. I can't pretend you don't love me. I can't act like we never met." His lips parted, but no words came out. His gaze rested on my face and looked grieved. I didn't know what else to do so I pulled him to me, clutching him tighter in my arms. After a few moments, I loosened my grip and kissed his temple. "Tell me how you're here, but you're not here. I don't understand." He looked away from me, and tried to step back, but I wouldn't let him. "Collin. Tell me."

"It's a Valefar power. It was the only way I could see if you were really here. I used the bond to track you to this point. You were so scared earlier that it wasn't hard to find you. The bond is more intense when you're afraid. After that, the bond paled, so I thought it was a vision and you were gone again. But the bond didn't completely break off." He swallowed hard. "I'm not really here. For me it's like a dream. My real body is hidden below. What's in front of you is a manifestation of dark magic."

"I don't understand. Why didn't you teach me to do this when you showed me how to use my Valefar powers? What did you do to yourself?" My eyes lingered on his face. Dread crept up my throat as his silence became longer and longer. "Collin...?"

"I didn't teach you because it would have corrupted you further. It's an acquired power. One that can be used when the right things are within reach. It requires a sacrifice. Blood." He closed his eyes. "With enough demon blood, a Valefar can split in two. The second body, this one, becomes whatever I want. It looks like whoever I want, says whatever I want, and sounds the way I want. It leaves my true body, and is typically used to lure prey back to the Valefar. It has risks that most wouldn't attempt, but I had to. I split myself, and made myself look and sound like the Collin you saw three months ago. But this body is a shell and will dissipate as soon as I release the magic I'm using—or I become too weak to maintain it. And I'm weak Ivy. You'll start to see what I look like now. What they've done to me."

I couldn't breathe. The horror of what he did choked me. A sacrifice? What did he do? Months ago, he willingly took my place and endured agony since then, just to warn me to turn back now. I'd pushed him farther into this by making him come looking for me. No words would form in the storm of thoughts battling through my mind. Instead, I reached for his face and pressed my lips against his. When he didn't resist, I pressed my body harder to him, wrapping my hands around his neck. My tongue traced his soft mouth, as his lips parted and I kissed him deeper. My heart raced in my chest. Warm tears streaked down my cheeks. His thumbs brushed through the tear trail, and then Collin's lips moved to trace the path down my cheeks. He gently kissed the tears away. Then he pressed his lips softly against each closed eyelid. He pulled me against his chest and kissed the top of my head. I could hear his pounding heart as he held me close.

"I'll help you as much as I can," he said. "But, I have to be careful. If they notice what I've done, they'll know you're here." I nodded. "Ivy, nothing is as it seems down here. Be especially careful of anyone who claims to be me. Run from any place that is beautiful. Beauty doesn't belong down here. Soon, you'll come to a beautiful forest. You'll see what I mean when you get there. Vile creatures live there. Remember that demons aren't the only things that can kill you down here. Just about anything can tear you to shreds." He pulled me away from his chest, and tilted his head. "Did you say you kicked the Guardian's ass?" A crooked smile slid across his face.

I nodded, smiling slightly. "Yeah. He's blind with severe dental problems right now." I held up the tooth shard that I'd kept.

Collin looked at it and then back at me with his mouth hanging open. "Is that one of its teeth?" he asked wide-eyed. I nodded and explained to him what happened as quickly as I could. As I spoke I could see Collin's skin discoloring in places. Red wounds and black bruises washed over his skin like watercolors. Welts appeared on his body containing long lacerations. His brilliant blue eyes faded into sunken dark orbs. His strong muscles and smooth skin began to melt away revealing a boy who'd been beaten beyond recognition.

My throat tightened as I spoke. I wanted to pretend not to notice, but I couldn't. They were torturing him. I swallowed hard, as I reached for his hollowed cheek, "Collin...I'll get you out." He smiled weakly, kissed my forehead, and vanished like mist in the sun.

CHAPTER SEVENTEEN

My feet were dragging, scraping against the stones as I followed where the bond pulled me. The cawing of birds still echoed around me. Cries of animals rang out in the distance. I wasn't alone down here, but so far I'd only heard sounds, and felt breezes as the Underworld creatures moved quickly around me.

I was so drained that I could hardly stand. Moving my legs took overwhelming effort. The desire to sit down and cry consumed me, but I couldn't give in to it. I had to keep going. I wrapped my arms around my middle as I walked, thinking about how Collin's arms held me tightly not so long ago. The memory of his skin on mine was still vivid. It warmed me inside to think about it. But, when I saw what he really looked like before he disappeared, before the magic wore off and he was forced back to the cell below, I couldn't bear it. Pressing my eyes closed tightly, I tried to shake the utter agony painted on his face from my memory. But it didn't recede. It was etched in my mind, always returning to the front of my thoughts.

Anger coursed through me, mingled with despair. Collin was older than me. Wiser. He knew what he was getting into. I didn't. And it didn't look like he could survive whatever they were doing to him much longer. What made me think I could? Hoping not to get caught seemed like a stupid plan. If I did get caught, I knew my fate would be worse than Collin's. But, I couldn't leave him. Just look at what they did to him! Abandoning him was something I couldn't do, even if I got my ass handed to me. Even if I risked everyone and everything else to do it.

As I walked through the Underworld, it was becoming clearer that the only way for me to save Collin was to defeat Kreturus. When I first thought about rescuing Collin, I thought I could sneak in, take him, and sneak out. I didn't have more of a plan than that, and it seemed good enough. But now, I knew there would be a confrontation. There was no way Kreturus would allow me to leave. And if I wanted to leave with Collin, it would be a fight to the death. A chill ran over my skin, and I pulled my arms tighter to my body. I had no idea how to fight a demon. If I saw Kreturus right now, I'd die. I was sure of that. How do you fight an ancient demon? One that was so powerful, even the Martis couldn't contain him forever? But, somehow, that's what I was supposed to do. That damn prophecy actually made me feel a little better. It was the only thing that said I could destroy Kreturus. It was the rest of the prophecy that I wanted no part of.

The path I was following had been dingy brown, illuminated by glowing rocks that resembled dying embers. Nothing changed. The Underworld looked the same since I left Apryl at the Pool of Lost Souls. I took one step, and then another, as hopelessness washed my pride away. It was several minutes before I realized what I was looking at. The scenery had changed gradually, becoming lighter and brighter until I stopped before massive trees. Their trunks were as wide as houses, and they gleamed silver, stretching up hundreds of feet into the air. The leaves made a dim chiming sound as they moved. My eyes darted from tree to tree, looking for something in the branches high above me that caused the limbs to shake, but there was nothing.

Uncertain, I stepped forward, knowing I had to pass this way. Collin said to beware of the forest; to beware things of beauty in this place. This forest of silver more than qualified. It was stunning. I wanted to stop and admire the delicate silver leaves and their intricate filigree. Each leaf appeared to have a different pattern cut into the silver, resulting in a different toned chime when the leaves shook. Clusters of gemstones grew at the tree's base in vibrant jewel tones. Little golden flowers sprouted up all over under the canopy of silver. They looked like little golden buttercups. I stood there in awe, staring at the forest in front of me. Its beauty was unreal.

Just then, my neck prickled. But, when I looked behind me no one was there. My pulse shot up a notch, and I kept walking. The trees would rustle and then fall silent. It happened over and over again. And it was oddly quiet in the silver woods. The cries I'd heard earlier must have been completely muted by the massive trees. It spooked me. Forests usually housed life and have the noises to let you know. This forest was silent, save for the jingling of the metal leaves. It felt wrong. As I walked deeper into the woods the feeling of eyes watching me didn't dissipate. Instead the feeling grew stronger. My eyes darted from silver tree, to golden bush, and back again. There was nothing there, but my stomach churned and the prickling sensation on my neck wouldn't go away. Finally, I stopped and turned. My heart was thumping in my chest. The muscles in my legs twitched, ready to run. It seemed like something was following me at a distance for a while. But, now it was close. Very close.

Peering into the trees, I finally saw what was following me. A small black bird sat high above me on a branch. It sat there, looking like a spot of ink against the ethereal silver canopy. Its black feathers gleamed with a purple tint. Its razor sharp beak sat below black staring eyes. Its head twitched from side to side, but its eyes remained locked on me. It was a grackle. Smiling slightly, I looked at it and felt stupid. Birds didn't scare me and this bird was tiny—smaller than a crow. What could it possibly do to me? My nerves were running on empty. I couldn't believe a bird spooked me. I laughed nervously to myself as I turned to start walking again. But then my breath caught in my throat and I nearly choked. There were hundreds of them. No, thousands. Grackle bodies lined so many of the silver branches that they formed a black wall.

The first grackle I saw made its horrible call. The high pitched screech shattered the silence. Suddenly, the birds swooped from their perches, extending their black wings, and dove at me. My arms shot up to cover my head, as my feet hit the path hard and fast as I ran. Several of the birds dive-bombed me, snipping at my skin with their sharp beaks during each pass. I screamed as one tore through my hand. Blood dripped from my arm, but I didn't dare stop to see the damage. I ran. These birds were trying to rip me apart. They seemed to savor the taste of flesh. Another bird nipped my leg, tearing a piece of flesh away. A wild scream sprang from my throat. My heart pounded so violently that I thought it would explode. I ran so fast, and scared out of my mind that I didn't notice the change in the forest. I passed splintered silver trees, and jumped over fallen logs that blocked my path. The little golden flowers were dug up, and wilted. Many of the trees had holes in their branches, like a Mac truck had driven straight through them. Another scream tore from my throat as more grackles tore at the flesh on my arms.

Suddenly the birds stopped. It was like they flew into a strong gale and couldn't come farther. I slowed after the grackles withdrew. They landed in the damaged trees, squawking like deranged demons. Not one bird left its perch to peck at me. Why did they stop? What were they afraid of? Oh crap. What would make flesh-eating birds retreat from easy prey? Turning slowly, I knew it had to be behind me—something that frightened those birds—something that was much worse.

Looking around, I finally noticed the crushed landscape. Trees laid in piles, splintered from their massive trunks. The forest floor looked as if it had been dug up and thrown askew. Clumps of dirt were everywhere. But it was what was in the center of the clearing that concerned me. Several trees were clustered together forming a silver ring. It looked like a nest; a gigantic silver nest. I stared at the spaces between the downed trees. Large red eyes stared back. Through the silvery foliage I could see dark scales surrounding those horrid red eyes, accompanied by a massive yawning maw filled with pointed teeth. My eyes grew wide. I suddenly stopped breathing. It was a dragon! And it wasn't just any dragon; it was the dragon from my vision. The one that killed me. I froze. Nothing happened. Nothing moved. It was like time stopped and we just stared at each other. Whatever chance of saving Collin that I thought I had shattered and blew away. This beast would kill me. I was certain of it.

So far, it hadn't moved. It lay there, staring at me. I slid my foot backwards slowly like I was backing away from a rabid dog. I hoped it wouldn't move. But, I had no such luck. As soon as I started to drag back my other foot, a grackle decided I was close enough, and dove at my arm. Its razor sharp beak tore through my skin, and its claws yanked a chunk of hair from my head. I swatted at it, yelling, until it flew away. Clutching my arm, I looked behind me. The grackles were still there, eerily quiet, watching me—waiting for me. And in front of me was a dragon. My options sucked. Go back and be attacked by a flock of demon birds. Or go forward and risk facing whatever scared the grackles enough to let their meal walk away.

I didn't get to decide. The red eyes flew straight up into the tree canopy, followed by a massive black body covered in glimmering scales. The dragon's talons were black like brimstone, its enormous maw filled with razor sharp teeth. A long tail hung down from the branch where it perched, stopping several feet above the ground. Before I realized what I was doing, my feet were moving. I shot under the branch and ran out the other side. The dragon bellowed that horrible sound that I heard in my vision. The ground shook as the tree where the dragon was perched came crashing down. It let out another cry and bounded off the ground and into the air. The sound of metal scraping metal made me turn. The beast was retracting its claws over and over, as its enormous black veined wings propelled it faster and faster towards me. If it had been able to shoot off the branch at top speed, it would have caught me already. My feet pounded the uneven terrain as I neared the edge of the forest. Its wings forced gusts of air against my back, it was so close. But, I didn't slow down. I didn't turn to see that it was near enough to breathe down my neck. The vision I had of the dragon was still vivid, and there was no doubt in my mind that this was the creature that I saw slicing Collin and I into a million pieces.

The edge of the woods was in sight. I hoped to God that the beast was bound to reside within the forest. Otherwise there would be no way to escape it. I'd have to turn and fight. And I'd die. How the hell do you fight a dragon? I only had that tiny comb. Its scales were larger than my hand. What would a little comb do? Nothing!

Fear burst though me giving my muscles another spurt of energy, but I wasn't fast enough. The dragon's wings were pressed tightly to its body as it shot from the sky and straight towards me at top speed. Its maw was open as it made an ear-piercing cry. The cry sounded like a distant echo, muffled by the pounding terror of my own heart, growing louder as it rapidly closed the distance between us. Panting, I tried to think of what to do. The beast wasn't stopping. It sounded more agitated. More horrifying. I'd have to turn to fight it, or it would rip me to shreds from behind. My fingers faltered, trying to grab my comb from my hair and extend the tines, but I didn't get the chance. An arm grabbed me, pulling me into a patch of underbrush. I screamed, fighting the hands that yanked me to the ground.

"Shut up," Shannon scolded me. "It's just me." I dropped to the ground, lying face-down in dirt so I could see what was happening.

Eric had jumped onto the path when Shannon pulled me off, and held up his palms. The dragon looked even more pissed off than before, and extended its black talons at Eric's head. The brilliant flashes of blue light that emanated from Eric's palms were instantaneous. The beast reared up, exposing its scaly underbelly to Eric, and cried out slashing it pointy claws blindly. As the light grew brighter still, Shannon started to pull me toward the clearing ahead. The light pulsed from Eric's hands like a strobe. With each flash he took a step backwards, until the dragon retreated. It was obvious that the beast didn't like the blue light. I wasn't sure if the dragon hated the brightness of it, or if Eric was using his Martis powers to do something else. Either way, it was working. After one last bright surge of light, the beast flew off smacking into trees and splintering off huge chunks of silver as it passed.

I doubled over, trying to get enough air to speak. Eric reached us and looked relieved to see me. He grinned, "You can't keep it no matter how much you beg. Dragons are not pets, Ivy." He laughed.

I sucked in air, still too tired to speak, and punched him in the arm. "You jerk," I laughed, still panting. "I thought those birds were going to kill me, then I ran straight into that dragon. How did you know it didn't like light?"

He shrugged, "Most creatures down here don't. I was too stunned to try and use it at the Pool before. Not to mention that it's not that discreet. It's like waiving the Martis flag down here. It's possible that others will know we're here now. Blasting Martis powers around down here isn't exactly inconspicuous." He sighed and looked at me. "I thought we might not see you again. I screwed up at the Pool of Lost Souls. I thought I saw…"

"It's all right. There was no way to know," I said looking away from him.

"But you must have seen Collin, right?" I nodded. He stepped in front of me, forcing me to look up at him. "But, you didn't walk into the water. I did. I never expected to see her again. It was like being sucker-punched in the worst way possible. I couldn't breathe. I couldn't think. It was just Lydia…and me. I would have been trapped there if you didn't step in." He smiled weakly at me. It was a humble smile. It must have been weird for a warrior to be saved by me. Eric was the one who trained me, and knew first-hand that my mad fighting skills were non-existent. I just got lucky. A lot.

"Don't even go there," I smiled, walking past him. Humble hero; that was an oxymoron. I was glad to see him again. And that he and Shannon were together. It bothered me a little bit that they didn't wait for me, but with those demon birds flying around, a dragon, and God knew what else—it made sense that they didn't wait. "I'm just glad to see you guys again. What happened? Where did you guys go? I started to think you turned back."

His eyebrow shot up. "No, we didn't turn back. Shannon dragged me away from the Pool. She left me to recover and then ran back to get you. Then those birds came and separated us. I couldn't find Shannon or you. So, I kept walking. The paths were twisting and I had no idea if I was even going the right way."

Shannon continued, "Same here. When I went back for you, those stupid birds dive-bombed me. I never got to you. I had to run. And when I ran back for Eric, he was gone. After I ditched the evil birds, something was herding me. I couldn't see it, but I could hear it above me. Once in a while when I didn't know which way to go there was an ominous black mass on one of the paths... so I chose the other one."

Eric was nodding, "Me too. That dragon was trailing us, pushing us back together."

"So he could eat us all at once," Shannon said, shivering. "Did you see the claws on that thing?"

I nodded. "Yeah. I saw them." A grackle screech startled me into motion. "We need to keep moving. Stopping makes the evil things down here think we're a buffet."

Shannon walked quickly ahead. "I hate those birds," she said as she quickened her pace. I hung back a few steps, walking behind her with Eric. He was quieter than usual and had his hands shoved in his pockets.

Lines creased his forehead as he looked at the ground. His voice was soft, "Ivy, I'm sorry... "

I cut him off. There was no need for apologies. I saved him. He saved me. Besides, long apologies made me uncomfortable. "Eric, it's fine. We're all alive, and we found each other again. That's all that matters." I smiled at him.

His golden eyes slid to my face. They looked plagued with pain. There was no trace of a smile, no hint of the lightness that was usually so transparently Eric. His voice was a whisper so Shannon couldn't hear. "I feel like I've just relived the worst day of my life. Losing her once was bad enough. Ivy, I don't know how you're still standing. You've had more than enough shocks today too, but you keep going."

I looked at him puzzled, "Eric, what choice do I have? Give up and die? That's not really a choice."

"No, it's not," he agreed. And we began walking again. I didn't turn around to watch the silver forest shrink into the distance. I could feel the dragon's eyes still following me, waiting for another chance to rip me to shreds.

CHAPTER EIGHTEEN

Shannon walked in front, leading the way through the winding Underworld. It appeared to stretch on forever. We were back to trekking over rocky rust-colored terrain. The bond was weak, but it still pulled me forward. The weakness of it worried me. Did that mean that Collin was worse? I didn't want to think of what it would mean if the bond totally disappeared.

Eric broke the thought when he finally spoke. "I never told you about her. I figured the past was the past, why talk about it? But seeing her again made it feel like it just happened." I looked over at him. He stared straight ahead as he spoke, with his golden eyes fixated on the ground in front of us. "I was glad I was turned Martis. It was the only way to kill the bastards who stole her from me. I was born in the ancient world and things were different. I spent my childhood by the sea, along a trade route in the Mediterranean. I remember seeing the traders that sustained my tiny town. They brought the things we needed and traded on their way to the major ports. We were literally lodged between two huge cities, well, huge for then." He smiled. "I liked my village and my life. I didn't have much, but I loved what I had.

"Then odd things started happening. No one noticed at first. We thought a girl ran off and eloped, or a young man had hopes of being a trader and left the village behind. But, it wasn't true. With each passing day another person disappeared, and it was as if they never existed at all. They simply vanished. The attacks were becoming more widespread and more frequent." He smiled softly, "Lydia was a strong woman for a sixteen-year-old. Her hair looked like black silk. And her eyes…Her dark eyes were perfect. She rarely said anything about her fears, but with another villager snatched in the night even the strongest people were terrified. Myself included.

"We didn't know what evil could attack and disappear without a sound. Some thought it was evil spirits, while others thought it was raiders. Our village didn't have gates or walls to keep enemies out. Before then, there was no need. We were a small town on the coast of a Mediterranean trade route. Ships stopped to rest, traded, and were on their way. That was how we survived. But soon, every stranger was a suspect—every trader a possible demon. And, the attacks were not like the ones we'd seen in the past. There might have been a fight over land, or something that made sense. These didn't. Those being abducted had nothing in common—not status, appearance, or family. The evil struck at random, when we least expected. And without a body left behind, there was no evidence as to what happened." He took a deep breath to steady his voice. The horribly vacant expression in his eyes hid a tremendous amount of pain buried beneath his calm façade.

Eric glanced at me out of the corner of his eye and continued, "After a while it was obvious that we were being attacked. People moved through the streets cautiously, and there was an unnatural silence that fell over us. We went on with the daily routine of things, and did what had to be done. But no one stayed out after dusk.

"I remember sitting with Lydia, as she rested her head on my shoulder. We looked out across the water. The sunlight glistened on the surface like precious stones. After everything that happened, that's still the memory that stands out the most. It was the last time we were together. Our wedding was four days away, and we thought we'd have a lifetime together. But things didn't work out that way. I had no idea how much I would lose before sunrise the next day.

I slid my fingers along her bare arms, enjoying the smoothness of her skin." He laughed, "That was risqué then. It thrilled me to push the line just a little bit. Ivy, I couldn't wait to be married, and have her as my wife. To hold her every night, and make sure she was safe. To provide for her and start our family. Lydia was my life. Everything. And I lost her. I lost everything in one careless act." Eric's feet slowed so much that he was barely moving.

I touched his shoulder gently, "Eric, you don't have to talk about this."

"It's not like that, Ivy. It's more like how did I get here? I'm walking through Hell with you and Shannon. The Martis condemned me to die. I'm a traitor to my own kind. Meanwhile, my entire life has passed and I have no idea how I got here. It started that night with Lydia. It stems back to her death. I'm here with you now, because of what happened then." He shrugged. "You have a right to know who I am. I screwed up. The last woman I swore to protect died in front of me, and I was powerless to help her. Then seeing her again…My God, Ivy, it feels like I'm reliving the same nightmare. How can I possibly protect you? I'm out numbered and out matched, just like I was then."

A confused mass of thoughts slid through my mind. Was he comparing me to Lydia? Why would he do that? Even with the circumstances as they were, I didn't see what he saw. But Eric was acting like he was ready to crack, and it stemmed back to Lydia. I didn't want to ask. I didn't want to know what happened to her or what he saw. This was the side of Eric that he kept hidden, neatly packed away beneath pressed shirts, and creased jeans. I don't know if it was stupidity or curiosity, but I asked anyway, "What happened to her?"

He pressed his lips together. I was uncertain if he was going to answer, but eventually he did. "I was mortal and weak. Those last few nights I watched her family's home without sleeping. I felt like if I watched, then I could do something if the time came. But when the time came, there was nothing I could do. I wasn't strong enough. In the end it didn't matter that I was there at all." His eyes stayed fixed on the ground as we walked. He shoved his hands in his pockets as his face took on a completely vacant stare. "A man appeared that last night. He walked into her house like he owned it, and emerged moments later cradling a limp body in his arms. Dark hair fell over his arms from the lifeless form, and I knew it was her—Lydia. I ran out at him with a blade in my hand. He laughed at me, brushing off my stab wounds like they were flea bites. I realized that he wasn't going to stop, and I couldn't let him go. I attacked again, jumping onto his back and dragging the blade across his throat. He should have crumpled to the ground covered in blood. Her body should have fallen from his arms. But, it didn't. Instead, he turned and grabbed me by the neck and dragged me with them. Lydia was still breathing, but she didn't look right. At first I thought she'd passed out, but that wasn't it.

"The man met up with a friend, at which point I was knocked out. When I came to, the only sound I could hear was Lydia's scream tearing from her throat. She was still alive and fighting, but it was no use. There were two of them. She tried to run, but they caught her, laughing like it was a game. They used her body," he swallowed hard as his face contorted into sheer hatred, "and when they were done, they drank her soul. That was the first time I saw a Valefar. The first time I witnessed a demon kiss. And it was done to my..." he didn't finish.

"How'd you survive?" I asked. "You weren't Martis yet, right?"

Eric shook his head. "No, I wasn't. I didn't know anything about any of this. I thought they were demons. After they killed Lydia they came at me. They untied me, and beat me. I lost consciousness a few times. It was like a cat playing with a mouse. I got smacked around for their amusement, and when they got bored they'd end it. At that point rage flooded me. I wanted them to die. I wanted to hurt them until every last drop of sanity left their bodies in an agonizing scream. But, I didn't get the chance. An old woman came across us. She acted like the two Valefar like they were nothing, and chased them off. After that, she took me in, healed my wounds, and my mark appeared a few days later." Eric's rigid stance suddenly deflated and his shoulders slumped. The lines of hatred that twisted his face had washed away, as he glanced at me out of the corner of his eye.

"It was Al, wasn't it?" I asked. What other crazy old woman would it be?

He nodded. "She healed me, told me what I'd become—a Martis. She trained me. It took every shred of patience that I had not to chase after the Valefar who killed Lydia, until I was certain I could destroy them. When I found them later, Ivy…" he paused looking at me out of the corner of his eye, "I couldn't punish them enough for what they did to her. Tormenting them wasn't enough. It didn't heal anything inside of me. Instead, it just ripped everything open again. Al said that I'd have an innate need to kill Valefar, but with those two, I resisted—tormenting them, keeping them alive until they begged for death. I learned to control my Martis urges long ago, but the damage the Valefar did—I didn't heal. I couldn't get past it. There's never been another woman, not in all this time. And seeing her. Here. My God. For a moment, I thought she was a Valefar. I didn't know how I'd…" he stopped and turned to me, just then realizing what he was about to say. He still harbored an enormous amount of disgust and hatred toward the

Valefar, but at least now I knew why. "Ivy, I'm so sorry. I meant that I thought I'd already seen the worst that could have possibly happened to her. I thought I knew the worst of what happened to her, but..."

I held up my hand, not wanting to discuss it. Demon blood was dirty. I already knew he thought that. I already knew that on some level, he despised me because of it. Of course that would be worse than death to a Martis. So I said, "I know what you mean."

By now Shannon was irritated that we were having a prolonged conversation without her. She was walking faster with her arms folded. It was a classic pissed-off Shannon stance. She could go ahead and be mad. I didn't care. It wasn't my story to tell, and he didn't tell her. He told me. "Come on. We better catch up with her before she starts jogging."

Eric grabbed my wrist to stop me. "Ivy, I feel like I have to protect you. Like it's what I was destined to do. But, I have no idea how." His eyes shone bright gold as he stared at me.

I don't know if he thought I'd condemn him for his bloodlust, but I couldn't. Not after living through a demon kiss. Not after seeing my sister turned into a Valefar. Rage and vengeance had become my allies when there was no one else. But, there was something else revealed in his past too. He was shattered and hardened. He learned to control his Martis instincts for his own satisfaction. And, he was as screwed up as I was. Those golden eyes were locked on my face, staring at me with complete hopelessness. Swallowing hard, I couldn't take it anymore. This wasn't a time to be gentle. We had no time.

Shaking my head, I said, "Eric, you're not reliving the past. I'm not Lydia. I'm the most powerful being between the Martis and the Valefar combined. The fact that you're here—that you and Shannon came with me—means more than I can say. And I know I didn't give you much choice. I got you into this. You're right. You're here because of me. Hell, everyone is here because of me!

Apryl wouldn't be here if she wasn't my sister, and Collin wouldn't be here if he..." suddenly I lost all my steam and my eye lids felt like lead. "It's my fault... " My body crashed to the ground as I felt the vision coming, but this time—everything changed.

CHAPTER NINETEEN

My lungs burned as I gasped for air. When the black mist cleared, I was on my hands and knees. It felt as if my ribs were being crushed like a soda can. I shook my head, trying to get my bearings...trying to stand and shake off the disequilibrium that the vision brought. But, it was no use. I fell to the floor and found my cheek colliding with cold dirt. My fingers clawed at the earth, trying to escape, but something pinned me. I couldn't get up. When I finally stopped struggling, the pressure on my ribs let up and I could breathe again. But as soon as I tried to stand, the process repeated itself. I learned quickly that my visions had changed. In the past, I felt like I was watching the vision from a distance. It was something that hadn't happened yet and most of the scene revealed to me was lost in shadows. I couldn't see everything. Now it felt like I was in the vision. My surroundings were crystal clear. All of them. I didn't have the impression that I was watching from a distance. No it was more like I was living in the vision. Did that mean I was in the present? Or the future? And things could hurt me now, and they were. I didn't know what happened, where I was, or what to expect.

Heart pounding, I scanned the room for any signs of life. It felt like I was in a closet. The entire room was filthy and masked in shadows. The air smelled rancid, like rotting meat. I tried not to gag on the stench. I wasn't able to turn my head, so I just scanned everything, trying to take in every detail. There wasn't much to see. The place was disgusting and terrified me. Bad things happened here. There was a feeling of death and decay that reeked in this place. My eyes were wide as I looked around, trying to figure out where I was. Through the shadows I saw his prone form, with sapphire eyes silently staring at me.

Collin's position was mirroring my own. One hand was outstretched over his head, as he lay motionless on his side. His beautiful face was slashed from temple to chin. A long bloody gash severed his lower lip. The clothing he wore when he came to me last was still on his body, but covered in filth clinging to him like a second skin. The dirty fabric hid more scars beneath. One bloody lesion was caked with rust-colored scabs that oozed down his leg. The demons left no flesh untouched. He was brutalized on every inch of his body. There was no part of him unscathed, except for his eyes. His beautiful deep-blue eyes were still perfect.

Terror shot through me. I tried to move, but I was still pinned to the floor by an unseen crushing force.

The pressure on my ribs increased to an unbearable degree. I couldn't breathe. Dread surged through me and shot up my spine like ice. I sucked in a small gasp of air, trying to get to Collin when his consciousness brushed my mind.

Ivy. A tear rolled down his cheek, as he gazed at me.

Collin, I thought I could save you. I thought.... A warm trail of tears spilled from my eyes and I couldn't stop them. They pooled on the ground, under my face turning the dirt to mud.

Suddenly, a screech filled the air and a single grackle flew into the room. A demon that I didn't notice before jerked me upright and hauled me away like a rag doll. Tears streamed down my face, but my limp body was no longer under my command. The demon's talon's cut into my flesh, as he lifted me over his shoulder.

"Kreturus is ready for you, again, Ivy Taylor. This is the last time, so there is no more use having trash lying around." The demon whistled one sharp note.

The black grackle swooped past me, and slowly landed in front of Collin's unmoving face. It let out an ear piercing shriek, as its razor sharp bill parted. I watched in helpless horror as it cocked its head, and fixated its cold black eyes on Collin, slowly moving toward his face. Collin's steady blue gaze ignored the bird, and locked eyes with me until the grackle's black feathers obstructed his view. With one swift movement the bird darted its shining head straight down. Collin's voice cried out as the beak sliced through his eye.

The demon stopped before leaving the room. His voice rasped deep from his chest, "Watch Ivy Taylor. Watch the pain you created." Tears welled up in my eyes, as I tried to turn away. The demon's fingers grasped my skull and forced me to watch as the bird pecked at Collin's eyes until there was nothing left but bloody sockets. Sobs shook my body as I dry heaved onto the creatures back.

He laughed saying, "This is your fault. All of it. Remember that as Kreturus takes you as his bride. Remember you could have prevented this fool's fate. But you chose not to."

A scream ripped from my throat as my chest felt like it was torn in half. My back arched in a quick movement, and the demon dissipated into black mist, and the vision ended.

The sound of a shrieking scream filled my ears before I realized that it belonged to me. My back arched as I shot up off the cave floor and slammed into Eric. He staggered backward, and sat down hard. I shut my mouth, trying to swallow the rancid fear that was making my heart explode. Gasping, I finally slowed my breathing and got control over myself. Shannon sat next to me, with an odd expression on her face. Eric was across from me, where he sat with a bloody nose.

Shannon spoke first, "What was that? What happened, Ivy? It was like a vision, but...it wasn't."

Wide eyed, I stared at her, too horrified to speak. I bit my bottom lip until I tasted my own blood. Eric's voice made my head dart in his direction. He held a handkerchief to his nose, and dabbed as the last of his nosebleed stopped. The white cloth, covered in crimson made my pulse shoot higher. My breaths came in fast shallow pants, as I clawed backwards into the dirt. I had to leave. I had to get away. I didn't know what I just saw, but my body was telling me to run. Run now!

"Ivy," Eric reached for me, but I shook him off. Wide-eyed, and shaking, I backed away from him. Nothing he said registered. The only thing I could hear was my heart pounding in my ears. The only thing I could see was the look on Collin's face as the bird...

Terror shot through me in a relentless wave, and at the same moment Eric threw his arms around me. I screamed, and kicked trying to break away from him. His soft voice slowly broke through my panic, "Ivy. Calm down. Breathe. You're all right, Ivy. You're all right." He repeated the words over and over again until the fight went out of me and I hung limp in his arms. He lowered me back to the ground and sat next to me. Shannon approached slowly, but wouldn't come closer.

My eyes stung and my face was damp. I wiped at the tears with the back of my hand. When I finally collected myself enough to sound sane, I asked, "What happened to me?" I couldn't look up at Eric. From the look on Shannon's face, it wasn't good.

Eric's hand rested on my shoulder, but I couldn't look at him. "I don't know. You fell asleep, like you were having a vision. But you started writhing, and screaming. It was like something was crushing you. Shannon and I couldn't do anything. We couldn't wake you up or call you back. I dumped the rest of my water on you hoping it would work and reset things, but it had no affect." He paused. "Eventually, you stopped struggling. That was when it got weird."

I looked up, "What do you mean?" His face revealed nothing of how he felt about the last few minutes, but Shannon's spoke with utter certainty. Her green eyes were wide, and her sun kissed skin was white.

She said, "Your mark burned on your skin. It was like someone lit it on fire. Then the color started to shift, and glowed bright red. As soon as that happened, black mist circled your body and you began to fade. It was like the mist was taking you."

I shook my head, clutching my face. "This can't be happening. It can't be. The visions were the only Martis ability I had. It can't be gone. It can't turn into this! I don't even know what that was! And what I saw, where I went…" I couldn't finish. Tears streamed down my face as my throat tightened.

Eric spoke after a few moments. "Your shadow is back. That's a good sign." He tilted his head looking at me.

My eyebrows arched in confusion, "What?"

"It disappeared with the mist," he said. "Shadows are tied to the living. Valefar and demons don't have them. Valefar manifest shadows on the surface to hide themselves and blend in, but it's fake. Being stripped of your shadow is part of the curse of the Valefar. They tried to take you in this vision. I don't know how Kreturus did it, but he must know he can. How did you come back? After your mark burned, your shadow faded and your body began to dissipate. You were nearly gone. How did you get back?"

My eyes burned as I stared at him. This was too much. I couldn't take another step. I couldn't risk that happening to Collin. How did I think I could save him? I was risking everyone's lives. Sobs choked me as they tried to bubble up my throat, but I swallowed them whole refusing to cry. Crying couldn't help me now. Nothing could.

Shannon's slight hand touched my shoulder, making me jerk. "What did you see?" It was such a simple question, but there was no way I could answer. When I tried to draw the words to my lips, the sorrow in my chest sucked them back down. Eventually, I just shook my head at her. "Ivy, we can't help you if we don't know what you saw. Come on. Tell us. Anything." Her pale face pleaded.

I swallowed hard. My voice was faint, "There's no way out. The prophecy comes true. Collin is tortured and dies. And there is nothing I can do to stop it." Hysteria crept up my throat, choking me, as tears stung my eyes. "Can't you see? This was all for nothing! I risked everything and it won't matter in the end! It didn't matter at all. It's as if this was all planned and I walked straight into it." Eric and Shannon stood next to one another watching me. It felt like I was shattering and the tiny pieces that were left of me were being blown away. Every inch of my body stung as grief dug its nails further into my stomach. I smiled weakly at Shannon. "You were right all along. I wasn't supposed to come here. You said there'd be this guy and he'd damn us all. You said I'd do horrible things because of him. And here I am, Shan. Standing in the Underworld, throwing away everyone I cared about to save one person. One person who's already been tortured and beaten beyond recognition…because of me."

Shannon's mouth fell opened. I waited for her to say something that matched the shocked expression on her face. But she said nothing. When Eric's face contorted into the same expression, I knew they weren't looking at me anymore. Something was behind me. Warm breath cascaded over my shoulder, lifting my hair in the process. Neither Eric nor Shannon said a word. They remained perfectly still. I closed my eyes and knew what it was before I opened them again.

The dragon.

It had to be. That thing was following me the entire time I'd been down here. I just didn't know what to do if it was really that close. When I opened my eyes I swallowed hard. The enormous maw filled with rows of pointed teeth loomed inches from my face. The dragon's red eye was the size of a tractor tire, and fixated on me.

My body shook as I rose slowly, and stepped away from it. One step, then two. When it jerked its head, I stopped moving and stared at it, waiting for it to attack. I locked my jaw to keep from screaming out in fear. I stared. The dragon's eye was like a human eye, but held much more detail. Shades of crimson and scarlet mingled together making the beast's iris have a jewel-like appearance. Gleaming black scales surrounded its eyes in intricate patterns that I hadn't seen from further away. I stood there transfixed, waiting for it to act. I was certain this beast was hunting me, either for itself or for Kreturus. The dragon breathed slowly, creating a warm breeze that washed over me. Its breath didn't have the rancid scent that flooded from the demons' mouths. Instead it was slightly sweet, and had the faint scent of rain during a hot summer storm.

A massive paw slid forward, but the red eye didn't stray from my face. Eric started toward me, but the beast turned its head quickly, snapping at him. He froze where he was and didn't move. When the dragon turned back to me it lowered its head onto its paw, and appeared content to just watch me. I looked at Eric, not knowing what to do. Not knowing what it wanted. If it was going to kill me or carry me off, I thought it would have done so already. But it just sat there, looking at me. Its tail swooshed suddenly, and it felt like I was looking at an overgrown cat in reptile form.

"Eric..." I whispered, "what's it doing?" My body was starting to spasm from being so tense for so long. I tried to relax, but couldn't. The tension was making me twitch uncontrollably. The dragon saw the tiny erratic movements, but didn't move.

"I'm not sure, Ivy. That's Kreturus' dragon, right?" I nodded. It had to be. "I would have thought he was here to do something, but it seems content just looking at you." Eric's voice rose as he spoke. The dragon turned its head and growled at him. Eric's voice dropped to a whisper, "Can you walk away from it, slowly?"

The dragon's scaly lips parted and a thin beam of glowing red flame shot towards Eric. He jumped out of the way, and stopped speaking.

I shrieked when the fire poured over its lips. The dragon responded by closing its mouth, and looking back at me. Its eyes glittered in the darkness. I wrapped my arms around myself, trying to stop shivering. Biting my lip, I took a small step backwards. When the dragon didn't react, I took another. The entire time, my pulse raced at an ungodly rate and I was covered in sweat. I repeated one tiny step after another, all the time watching the enormous beast as I stepped away. The dragon didn't move. It didn't chase us. It just watched. When we were far enough away, I turned my back to it, but kept looking over my shoulder as we walked away.

"Kreturus. He knows we're here, doesn't he?" I asked them both.

Shannon's face showed her uncertainty. "I don't see how he couldn't. Not if that's his pet."

"I'm not sure it is," Eric replied. When I looked over at him, his face was pale and glistening. His shirt was soaked through with sweat. He shoved his hands in his pockets without looking at me. "If it was, it should have done something by now. That was the second time we saw it."

"It seems like it's been following me," I glanced back over my shoulder at the beast. Its form was a black speck. One moment it was there, and the next time I turned to look, it was gone. Its silent movements scared me, but Eric was right. Something wasn't right with that thing. "When we were separated, I felt like there were eyes on me at times, but couldn't see anything. But sometimes I heard his wings and felt their breeze brush across my face. That dragon seemed like it was trailing all of us. When the birds attacked me, it scared them off. It chased the grackles rather than me. Do you think it's possible that it's helping me?" I heard the doubt in my voice as I said it. Why would a creature of the Underworld help me? It made no sense.

Shannon shrugged, "Maybe, but I doubt it. Nothing's as it seems down here."

CHAPTER TWENTY

We followed the maze of paths through the cave. My sense of direction sucked on the surface and I could only hope that I was leading us in the right direction. I was relying on the bond. As we progressed deeper and deeper into the Underworld the bond changed. It felt like a burning hole that would consume me entirely if I didn't find Collin soon. Perhaps it was a hole. We shared the same soul. Each of us was bonded to the other in a way I didn't think was possible. I only hoped that I wasn't too late and that the last vision I saw could be altered, and didn't already occur. But my visions were getting weirder and weirder. The repetitive one with the dragon appeared three times, and always foretold the same horrible future. Its crushing talons meant the death of Collin and I, both. But, this last vision didn't make sense. It's almost like it wasn't a vision at all. I wished Al were here to ask, but she'd already told me that my powers weren't like anything she'd ever seen before. Unease chewed at me from within, as I wrung my hands.

Shannon glanced at me before she said, "You're still thinking about that last vision, aren't you."

I prickled at her words. "I'm not talking about it."

"I'm not asking you to," she said. She looked at me for a second before she continued, "I don't need details, Ivy. But, I would like to know how it changed from within the vision. Eric knows a lot of stuff. Look at him leading the way ahead of us like some deranged Boy Scout." A smile spread across her face as she laughed. I didn't mean to laugh at him, but the giggle escaped me in a swift snort as I tried to cut it off.

Eric looked back at us and murmured, "Girls behind me, and they are both laughing. Awesome." He flashed a smile and shook his head, as he climbed over a pile of stones that blocked our way. Shannon and I reached the rocks at the same time. I pretty much fell over them and slid down the other side on my butt.

"That's one way to do it," Shannon laughed. And Eric smiled at me, offering me a hand up. I grimaced at Shannon and took his hand. My jeans were so trashed. Did the Underworld have a GAP? I was covered in mud, dirt, blood, and guardian drool. A change of clothes seemed like a dream right then.

"Do you think we're closer?" Eric asked. I had no idea how big the Underworld was or how long it would take to reach Collin. But the bond seemed to change as I got closer. It was the only indication I had that we were making any progress.

"Yeah, we are," I answered. "I can feel him, but something's off. It's like the signal is getting botched. I'm not sure why." Eric's face was tired and covered in dirt. He ran his fingers through his hair and nodded.

Shannon patted my shoulder and stopped as the path forked again ahead of us. "Which way?"

I stood in the crossroads for a moment. It was not practical to stay still too long here, not if you valued your life. Unmoving objects tended to be devoured by grackles, dragons, or demons. The grackles could be heard looming in the distance, and there was never just one. I took a few steps down one path and then the other. The pull of the hollow spot in my chest, the place that the bond usually pulled, was silent. It didn't react to either path. I sat down hard, pushing my frizzing hair out of my face. "I don't know." This never happened before. I always felt something. There was always some indication telling me which way to go—a pull, a push, or a feeling. But not this time. Eric and Shannon stood watching me. "I'm sorry, but I don't know. I can't tell."

"It's not a problem," Eric said. "There was a pool a little ways back. I'll refill the water bottle. Sit and wait. You're exhausted." When Shannon came running in to warn us when we were in the catacombs, she'd had the foresight to grab a water bottle and several Powerbars. We didn't need much food, but we still needed some. Water was everywhere in this dank place, so refilling the bottle wasn't difficult. As Eric walked away, I sat and stared at the paths. My heart twisted, and I squeezed my eyes shut to prevent Shannon from seeing the pain etched on my face, but when I looked up at her, her gaze was following Eric. There was an expression on her face, and a softness in her eyes that I'd never seen in her before.

She broke her stare, and arched an eyebrow at me, "What?" She sat down next to me, and pulled her long hair over her shoulder. It was a nervous tick of hers.

A lopsided grin formed on my lips. "You like him. How did I not see this before? You like Eric!"

Shannon's spine straightened as she twisted her head towards me.

Her mouth fell open, but words were slow to form. "I...I don't like him like that. I just think he's— interesting." She shrugged and flipped her hair over her shoulder.

I laughed, "Interesting? A pork chop is interesting. That guy is a two-thousand-year-old Martis warrior. Interesting is the wrong word, Shan. Try again."

She sighed and cocked her head at me. "Fine. He's more than interesting. He's," she paused searching for the right words, "kind, honorable, and loyal."

"Loyal?"

"Okay, he's really hot. I like the way he walks, his lopsided smile, those amber eyes, and him. Okay. Just everything about him." She sighed staring down the path. This was a side of her that she rarely revealed. High school boys didn't impress her much. There was one other time she was love struck over some guy, but that was a while ago. She turned back toward me and arched an eyebrow. "So? Go ahead and say it?"

"Say what?"

"That he's not interested in me. It's okay. I can tell. That's the way things go, I guess. I finally find someone worth looking at and he seems more interested in you." She said the comment causally, like it'd happened before, but I had no knowledge of it ever happening at all. Never mind now.

"He does NOT like me. I just remind him of someone he was fond of." She looked skeptically at me, ready to say uh huh, but I cut her off. "It is not the same thing. Reminding someone of the past is just that—I'm reminding him of someone he cared about who's dead. He feels like he's seeing a ghost when he's around me. It's horrible. No, actually liking someone brings happiness—not hollowness and grief." I rolled my eyes at her. How could she even think that? I was starting to think that I didn't know her at all anymore. Could she change that much over such a short time?

Eric returned with water and handed me the bottle first. Shannon gave me a 'told you so' glare, and I rolled my eyes at her. Eric asked, "What'd I miss?"

Shannon jumped up and dusted herself off. Smiling at him she said, "Absolutely nothing. So which way, Sacagawea?"

"Are you Louis or Clark?" Eric laughed.

I stood, ignoring the two of them and walked towards the fork in the path again. The cavern ceiling divided the path in two, touching the ground and forming the largest stalactite I'd ever seen. Knowing time was a luxury I didn't have, I took another swig of water and shoved the bottle at Shannon. With my hands emptied, I walked over to the massive rock and ran my fingers over it. The bond pulled slightly, warming my chest and giving me hope. I pressed my eyes shut to savor the sensation. *I'm coming Collin. I'm coming.*

Shannon's voice cut through my thoughts, "Great. We have to go through the rock, right?" When I turned, her hip was cocked and her head tilted. I nodded at her.

Eric walked to the stone, and ran his fingers over it. "How? Do you really mean go through it—as in go inside of it? Or go over it?"

"I think we have to go inside of it." I dragged my fingertips along the cold damp stone. There was no entrance, no obvious door to walk through. The horrifying music of demon bird calls caught my ear, and Eric and I turned at the same time to see them coming in the distance.

"Grackles," all three of us said in unison.

"We've got to get out of here." Shannon said urgently, and started pressing against the rock. She slid her hands all over the stone, but nothing moved.

The ear piercing cries grew louder. "There's no time!" Panic raced up my spine in a cold flash. All three of us dragged our hands over the stone, looking for an entrance, but nothing appeared. My heart pounded faster in my chest. The memory of what those birds can do came back to me. Their cries made my skin crawl. Desperately we tried everything we could think of to open the rock. We had celestial silver, brimstone, and Apryl's necklace.

"The necklace!" Eric shouted. "It opened the crypt. Try it on the stone! Do it now!"

I pressed her necklace to the stone but nothing happened. The swish of a thousand wings echoed off the stone walls. My throat constricted as I looked over my shoulder and saw a mass of black beating wings. Their calls were so loud that I couldn't hear anything else. I couldn't even hear the rapid beating of my own heart. I screamed and slammed my hand against the stone, half clawing at it. The rock sliced my palm open, but I didn't care. The grackles and their scissor beaks were within a few feet of us. I pressed my face to the rock and tried to block out the spaces by pressing my arms and hands into the stone. Suddenly, the rock turned to sand and I fell through. Eric and Shannon followed. As we tumbled through the sand-like stone, the opening that swallowed us sealed. Silence washed over us as we stared at each other wide-eyed.

"What happened? What'd you do?" Eric asked.

Breathing heavily I stood, and looked at my palm. Without a word, I held it up. Apryl's necklace was in my palm, and covered in dark red blood. "It wanted blood, brimstone, and silver. Greedy rock." I meant it jokingly, but Eric nodded.

"Indeed. And you are certain we have to go this way?" Eric looked around. The cavern walls were paler, almost as if they'd been dry-brushed with gold. He swallowed hard.

I turned to see what was concerning him only to be confronted by a narrow golden passage. The floor was lined with sapphires. The walls were real gold with a dull luster. Etchings were carved into the precious metal revealing beautiful flowers with jewel-crusted centers. It was beautiful. It was beautiful. Oh no. My worried gaze cut to Eric for an explanation, but it was Shannon who spoke.

"This is the Lorren, isn't it?" Her fingers touched the golden wall gently. She turned back toward us with her eyes as big as emeralds.

"What's the Lorren?" I asked. "Where are we?"

She replied, "We're in part of the Underworld—the Lorren shows you everything you ever wanted, but never had. It's pure temptation. No one has passed through this tunnel and lived." Her gaze was wide, as her fingers pressed against a golden lily.

"How do you know that?" Eric asked. He walked briskly toward her, and she turned from the flower. His brow creased at the center when he asked again, "How did you know that?"

She flinched, unable to back away from him. I asked, "What's the matter, Eric? Why wouldn't she know that?"

He turned sharply, with an agitated expression, "Because only The Seeker knows that. Only the Seeker knows what the Lorren is, and how it traps the Prophecy One. I was supposed to use it to trap you, so you couldn't escape. No one escapes from this tomb." He turned back to Shannon. "Answer me. How did you know?"

Shannon tried to laugh it off, but Eric was in her face. She rested her hand on his shoulder, "Eric, it's not..." but he shook her off.

He was practically growling now. "Answer me. How did you know about the Lorren?"

She rolled her eyes, "Fine. I'm not as saintly as you, all right? Are you happy now? I overheard Julia talking about it. With you. I heard about the whole thing."

Eric's expression softened, but he didn't back away. "When?"

"I don't know," she answered annoyed. "It was some time last year before you knew you were tracking Ivy." She slid past him and looked to me for help. "Martis or not, I'm still a little bit of a snoop. How could I hear part of that conversation and keep walking? Ivy, come on. Tell him."

"She has a way of knowing everything and never getting caught." I shrugged. "Is that not a Martis-ie thing to do?" I knew it wasn't, but Eric seemed to think it was on the same level as something really bad.

"No, it's not." His amber gaze bore into Shannon's back. I reached for his arm, but he shook me off. He turned toward Shannon, "So tell us about the Lorren. Tell us why we can't pass this way."

Shannon's eyes shifted between Eric and me, but it was Eric she had to appease. He seemed very uneasy now. "It's what I said before. The Lorren can manifest temptations specific to the individual who passes through the tunnel. It will create the deepest desires that hide within your heart. The Lorren uses it to isolate it's victims, and leave them encased in gold in their fantasy forever. The carved flowers and gems on the wall aren't carvings, are they?" she asked him.

"No, they aren't." Eric replied.

My fingers had been touching a rose with a jeweled stem. I turned and asked, "What are they then? It has to be a carving. The image was stamped into the gold on the walls."

"Tell her." Eric said.

Shannon looked uneasy and walked away from him. She stood next to me and stared at the flower. "They were people. People who were trapped here. They became part of the tomb. It's part of the riches that lure new victims into the tunnel." I pulled my hand away, horrified. Each exquisite flower had been a person?

Eric nodded. "Victims thought they would be in ecstasy forever. They were given the thing that was most desirable—the thing that they longed for but didn't have. It's pure bliss at first." His gaze met mine and didn't waiver. "But at the last moment of consciousness, their temptations twist into a terrifying perversion of what they had desired. The victim's horror is frozen in time, as their body is devoured by the Lorren. When the Lorren is finished, the victim's remains are etched into the walls. That is what the Martis intended for you Ivy. That was the way to bind you so you could never return."

I swallowed hard as horror poured over me. "Eric, I did nothing to deserve this. How did the Martis send me here? How did they do this!" I was about to burst into tears.

He reached for my shoulder, as he bent to look me in the eye. "They didn't. The bond is pulling you through here. Why we have to come this way is unimaginable. I also don't know if we can follow you. I couldn't get past the Pool of Lost Souls. I know who will be waiting in the tunnel for me. I know what guise the Lorren will be wearing for me." His voice trailed off as his gaze shifted toward the golden tunnel.

Shannon said, "We'll go through together. That should help, right? As long as we keep putting one foot in front of the other, we should be able to walk out the other side. It's stopping and giving into the Lorren that will kill us. We can do this Eric. We're Martis."

"No," his voice was razor sharp and his eyes burned with anger, "I'm not. Not anymore. They cast me aside Shannon. They thought I turned on them. I may have angel blood flowing through my veins, but I'm not one of them. Not anymore."

We stood silent staring at Eric. Such an outburst was unusual for him. I wasn't sure what to say, but I had to say something. "Labels don't matter. You are who you are. You're Eric. And you can do this. You have the benefit of knowing Lydia will appear in there. You know it isn't her. This isn't like the Pool at all. That thing tricked you into thinking she'd been made a Valefar. She's not. She isn't down here, so whatever you see in the Lorren isn't her. You're insanely rational Eric. You can do this. Me on the other hand…God knows what I'll see." The thought sent a shiver down my spine.

Shannon snort laughed, "Of course you know what you'll see. It will be Collin. So you do the same thing. Tell yourself it isn't him, that he isn't in there, and keep walking. And if you don't, I'll pull you."

I gazed at Eric and could tell he had a better idea of how hard that would be than Shannon did. But what choice did we have? This was the way to get to Collin. We had to pass through it. "So, stick together and don't stop. We can do this." My words didn't convince me we'd succeed, but they solidified my resolve. And I wasn't spending eternity in the Lorren. Screw that.

Shannon walked in first with her dagger drawn. Eric followed next, with me at the rear. As we walked into the tunnel the etchings became more numerous and more elaborate. The golden carved flowers had cascaded in bunches, each with its own jewels nestled in the petals. My throat tightened, as I breathed in controlling breaths. *Beware beautiful things*, Collin had said. The Lorren was the most beautiful part of the Underworld that I'd seen yet, which meant it was the most deadly.

I slid one foot in front of the other, waiting for something to happen as we walked into the golden tunnel, but nothing did. From the looks of it, the Lorren was a circular tunnel made from gold. It looked like a long slender tube, large enough to walk through. Although we couldn't see the other end, it looked pretty straight forward—walk through the tunnel and come out on the other side. As we walked deeper into the Lorren, I looked at the flowers on the walls. They were people who didn't make it out. And the place was full of flowers. I swallowed hard. We had to make it out. Staying together was our only option. We all naturally closed any space between us. Shannon and Eric must have been thinking the same thing. Silence surrounded us. The sound of dripping water was gone. No grackle noises. No dragon's wings. Just the sound of our footfalls.

When we entered the Lorren none of us thought it was very large. We were wrong. None of the things Eric was taught prepared him for what happened. He was never supposed to step foot inside the Lorren. His job was to capture me, kill me, and leave my body here. When he refused, he turned his back on his own kind. I looked up at him. He was walking next to me now. We all inched closer to one another. My eyes were darting everywhere trying to foresee what was coming. What happened was so incredible; there was no way I could have seen it coming. The Lorren was more deadly than I knew, and I was about to learn why.

As we walked further into the Lorren, the golden flowers were plentiful. They rose off the walls like they were cast in gold, and not just carved into it. I touched the wall with my fingers thinking of all the lives lost in this place. My stomach sank as the air began to move gently through the tunnel. The three of us instinctively stopped. Shannon and I reached for our blades, but it didn't matter. It turns out that you can't fight the Lorren.

The gentle breeze became instantly violent, and spun me around before throwing me back into the shining wall. The room twirled as the wind forced us apart. Eric was ripped from my side. The wind hurled his body deeper into the Lorren and out of sight. At the same time, I heard Shannon's scream erupt and suddenly die. As I tried to peel myself off the wall, a shimmering gold curtain formed around me. I pushed forward, forcing one foot down at a time. The wind pushed me back. For every two steps I took forward, I was pushed back one. My long hair whipped about my face and stung my skin. Finally, I made it to the golden curtain. I pulled it back and looked through. The golden flowers seemed to sway as the violent wind died. The gale finally stopped, and it was utterly still. There was no trace of Eric or Shannon anywhere. They were gone. My pulse was thundering. I turned in a slow circle wondering what would happen. Would the Lorren attack me now? Would it send a fake Collin to finish me off? I had to get out of there, but the spinning made me uncertain of which way I'd come in. There were no landmarks, and all the flowers looked exactly the same.

"Eric! Shannon!" I called out. But, the only sound I heard was my own voice echo back like I was standing in an empty hallway. I breathed in deeply and ran through the golden curtain. Neither end of the tunnel was within sight. The wind had pushed me further into the Lorren before it tore us apart. I clutched my face.

This couldn't be happening! I knew staying still wasn't an option. Freaky things would happen if I stood still. The Lorren would seduce me if I stood still, so I chose a direction and ran. The narrow golden hallway turned and forked in separate directions. Fear clutched at my stomach as I realized that this was not a tunnel.

It was a maze.

I slowed my steps, looking at the fork in the golden path and wondering which way I should go. Each path was equally ornate and looked exactly the same. Golden flowers draped the walls as far as the eye could see. Not knowing what to do, I shook my head and chose a path. I walked past hundreds of golden flowers that were once living people. Now they were trapped in gold.

Forever.

Panic was choking me. I took off at a full run. It was only a matter of time until the Lorren presented me with a temptation that I wouldn't be able to refuse. But it didn't matter. This was going to be impossible. The Lorren wasn't a tunnel. I couldn't walk straight through. I never thought it would be easy, but I never thought I'd be trapped here. My fingers touched the petals of the golden flowers as I slowed down my pace. My eyes stung as tears tried to form, but I couldn't let them. I had to get out of here. Now. The problem was every path looked the same. Row upon row of golden vegetation and gleaming gemstones filled my eyes, but there was no way to know if I was getting closer to the exit. The only clue I would have is when the amount of flowers thinned out. And, where I was, they were still so thick that the flowers hung off the walls in cascading mounds. Desperate anger rose within me and I screamed. I wanted to punch something, but there was nothing to hit.

My fingers threaded through the golden jeweled flowers hanging off the walls. My muscles flexed in my arms needing to release tension. An impulse shot through me and I wanted to rip the golden flowers down, as if it could hurt the Lorren. But, I couldn't rip them away. They were people. Well, they had been people. If it were possible any of their humanity was still trapped within the flowers, I couldn't destroy them in a fit of rage. Turning slowly, I looked at the paths before me. I could do this. Just keep wandering until the leaves thinned. Then I would be out—either back at the beginning or at the ending.

My eyes glanced around cautiously. I knew what to expect in here. I knew what my weakness was. I knew what the Lorren would tempt me with. It would weave the perfect illusion, so warm and inviting that I'd never want to leave. Then the golden flowers would suck me into the wall and I'd be trapped like the rest of them. Collin's warning floated through my mind, the more beautiful—the more deadly. This place was stunning, dripping with beauty.

Dripping with death.

For hours I walked and did not hear or see anything. No noises carried through the golden vines. No voices resonated through the tunnels. I'd thought Shannon would call out at any time, or I'd hear Eric's voice, but it was silent. Moving forward, I wound around the paths going deeper and deeper into the maze. My friends would have to face their own hell and find their own ways out. We were all on our own.

It was then that I heard his voice; when I was at my weakest. The Lorren waited, learning me, tasting my fears. It was patient. Eventually I felt the bond tugging in my gut and pulling me through the maze. Not having a better plan, I followed its pull knowing damn well that Collin would be at the end of the path. What else would the Lorren do? It was a predictable trap. It had to be. Otherwise I was totally screwed, because I didn't have a clue what else could possibly make me want to stay here and die.

Death meant abandoning my friends and forsaking my sister. Valefar or not, she was alive and I intended to keep her that way. I swallowed the lump in my throat. Seeing her face had been a double edged sword. She'd become the very being I was trying to avoid—a Valefar. But, she was alive. That was all that mattered. I had to free her from the Pool. I had to save Collin. I couldn't get sucked into whatever was at the end of this path. The bond propelled me forward, turning me around corners, and through archways of golden flowers. My steps became more cautious and less frantic as the acidic taste of dread rose in my throat. Swallowing it back down, I paused. I could feel it. He was around this corner. I knew it was him. It had to be. Collin was my vice. He always would be. Inhaling deeply, I closed my eyes. I willed myself with my entire being to be strong enough to deal with whatever lay around the corner. Then I walked the final steps half hoping that it would be something else. I had no idea that what I hoped for was worse than anything I'd feared.

CHAPTER TWENTY-ONE

My breath caught in my throat as I rounded the golden corner. Collin stood there perfectly healthy. His eyes sparkled that brilliant blue, and that devilish smile that I adored spread across his lips.

It's not him, I thought to myself. That thing was the Lorren. Dim rust-colored light was spilling from the end of the tunnel, just over his shoulder. I was near an exit!

I moved slowly. My heart pounded in my chest more fiercely than when the dragon stood nose to nose with me. I had the brains to resist the dragon, but Collin? Breaking the alluring gaze he cast over me, I looked at the golden walls, the floor...anything except him. Collin shifted his weight onto one foot and stood blocking the path. As I neared him I slowed down realizing that I couldn't pass by him without touching him. My brain immediately registered that as a horrible idea and I withdrew a step.

Collin laughed, "After all this time, you're stepping away from me? No hug for an old friend? No...kiss?"

Swallowing hard, I spit out the words before they froze in my mouth, "You're not him. Step aside, Lorren, and let me pass. Otherwise, I'll make you." I had no idea why I threw that threat in there. It sounded good, so I did. Too bad for me that this Collin liked it.

He smirked, taking a step towards me, "You'll make me?" A smile spread across his entire face. I made the mistake of looking up and seeing the amusement there. It was the same expression Collin had worn so many times.

Looking into his face, I mustered the most calloused expression I could manage. I took two steps toward him and stopped. Confidence I didn't own flowed out of my mouth, "Yes, I'll make you. Move." I took another step toward him and Collin stepped back. The golden light in the Lorren played off his hair, making it appear lighter—almost as if it were kissed with strands of gold.

The corners of his lips tugged upward, "Then, make me, Ivy Taylor." He folded his arms across his chest, clearly amused with the idea. "Make me move."

This wasn't going the way I planned. I just had to pass him and I'd be free. I was so close. My fingertip rubbed my ruby slightly as I thought about efanotating to the other side. That would be simple and effective. But I didn't know what powers the Lorren contained. Was it possible that it drained powers? And I seriously doubted it masked Valefar powers. I thought Kreturus already knew I was in Hell, but I didn't want to send up a flare by using my powers. He'd know exactly where I was and at this moment, I was certain he didn't know. If he did, this place would be crawling with demons. No, I couldn't efanotate past this false Collin. I was freaked, but no powers came to me his time. My hair didn't flame out in purple tongues of fire. The Lorren seemed to drain creatures of power to trap them here. No, I'd have to pass him without using any magic.

He gestured his hands toward his body, "Come on, Ivy." His lips were twisted into a full smirk. "You couldn't make me do anything before and you still can't now. That's just how it was with the two of us…unless you wanna prove me wrong?"

He was trying to bait me. I ignored his words, deciding that shouldering him as I passed was my best option. I had to knock him on his ass, and not touch his skin. I'd melt if I touched him even though it wasn't really Collin. It made me wonder for a second if the Lorren felt like him. If it would treat me like Collin. The danger in those thoughts made me doubt myself. The longer I stayed around him, the foggier my brain got.

So, I launched my body at him, shoulder poised to connect with his stomach. The shot connected and I threw him across the floor. He didn't expect that, which helped me. But, Collin jumped to his feet quickly. Within a matter of seconds he had me pinned me to the floor. He hovered inches above me, trapping me in place. My heart raced in my chest, as I screamed at him. Nothing I did made him move. He didn't release his grip. If anything, it made him hold me tighter. After realizing that flailing and screaming in his face weren't working, I finally stopped. Breathing hard, I tried to look anywhere, except at him. He was gazing at me. I could feel his eyes on the side of my face. The rise and fall of his chest against mine was intoxicating. The mental haze that was forming thickened, making it more difficult to think.

Collin's face loomed nearer to mine. His warm breath slid across my cheek, as he whispered into my ear, "That was a dirty shot. Since when do you like to play dirty?" Every muscle in my body tensed. His words were dripping with innuendo. His fingers slid against the side of my face, turning me to look him in the eye. Oh God. Butterflies filled my stomach as I gazed at him. He felt like Collin. He sounded like Collin. Every time he spoke, every time the Lorren opened its enchanting mouth, I felt woozier. With every moment he held me beneath him the feeling that he was Collin intensified.

Only a very small portion of my brain was functioning at that point. All my senses were drowning in Collin. His scent, his touch, his beautiful face…and more than anything I wanted to taste him. The thought of feeling his kiss against my lips was so enticing that I couldn't stand it. One more word and I knew I'd kiss him. One more sexy glance from his dazzling blue eyes and I was toast.

So, I did the only thing I knew to do. My knee connected with his groin in one hard shot. Collin fell to his side and staggered briefly before reaching for me. I jumped up and ran past him, still feeling the seductive fog lingering in my brain. Collin, no, the Lorren—stop calling him Collin—was right behind me. My heart pounded in my chest with a mixture of passion and fear. Every inch of me felt like it was on fire. In part, I wanted him to catch and seduce me. That was the crazy part of me who thought that this thing was Collin. It was like he was polarizing my brain. The part that acted on lust and passion was dominating. The logical, rational part that did most of my thinking was buried under a pile of mental slush. My legs barely moved. I meant to run, but couldn't seem to get going. It felt like I was running in slow motion.

I didn't get more than a few steps away from him before his body collided with mine. We went sliding across the smooth floor and slammed into a golden wall. Stunned, I shook my head and tried to get away, but I couldn't. Collin was faster. My head was swimming like I drank too much. My arms and legs were moving like they were stuck in gelatin. I lay on the floor, flailing, trying to get up. But, he moved his body over mine, slamming his hips down on top of mine. I was pinned to the floor so tightly that I couldn't move. His knee pressed into my thigh, and his hands gripped my wrists, pressing them to the cold floor.

He breathed heavily in my face, "Do you still want to run?" His lips brushed my ear slightly, and I shivered. "Or did you just want me to pin you to the floor?" The more he spoke the harder it was to resist him. I pressed my eyes closed trying to tune out his words, but I couldn't. The sound of his voice was like a siren song. The more I heard it, the more I wanted to stay and hear his rich, beautiful voice. It felt so good to be near him. Having him so close was pure bliss. I could stay like this with him forever. His body felt so hard and smooth, right on top of mine. I didn't want to free myself from his grasp. I wanted him with me, cradling my body in his arms. A warm kiss slowly grazed my cheek as Collin's lips touched me ever so slightly, teasing me.

The woozy feeling increased. I made the mistake of opening my eyes. Collin's lips lingered right above mine. His warm breath washed over me. His heart raced in his chest. I could feel it beating in sync with mine. A seductive smile appeared on his lips. I sighed, unable to look away from him, and buried my face in his neck. His strong arms pulled me tighter into him. I couldn't get close enough. It felt like I was so far away. So far away from Collin. *Collin.* My clouded brain was trying to communicate with my body. It was shooting off *Danger! Run!* messages, but I ignored them. My fight or flight response was totally broken. A giggle spilled from my lips instead.

Collin released one of my wrists, and ran his fingers through my hair. "I love it when you laugh like that." He pressed his cheek to my head and inhaled deeply, before lightening the pressure on my wrist and legs. I didn't try to run. Nothing could force me from his arms. I smiled, and pressed myself closer to him completely content to lay in his arms forever. He held me quietly for a little while, stroking my hair and kissing my face softly. When he spoke, every ounce of desire within me burned like I'd never known. Three simple words ignited me. "Kiss me, Ivy."

I liked that idea. Kiss him. Taste him. Hold him. Turning my face, I looked up at him. His blue eyes bore into me. It felt like he could see inside my soul. My soul. Why did that seem weird? It felt like he could see into my soul, but he couldn't. Why not? That should be normal. Collin could see inside of me. He knew what I felt and what I thought. The fog that clouded my mind wouldn't clear. I couldn't think. *Soul. Save.* My brain was fighting through the heavy haze that was obscuring my thoughts, but I didn't understand. The words alone confused me, but when a memory connected to the words, I could think better. *Kiss.* The memory of Collin and I in the old church flooded my mind. My sweat-soaked body. The stone floor. Anger. Rejection. Collin said he wouldn't kiss me that night. The idea terrified him. I remembered.

"Do you remember that night in the old church?" I asked him. "You said you couldn't be what I needed. What did you mean?" Something, a thought, was floating around in my mind just out of reach. Why couldn't we be together? I couldn't remember.

His voice was smooth and deep, "I can be what you need now. Kiss me, Ivy." He whispered in my ear, "Kiss me."

I shivered and felt the mental fog thicken again. The warnings my mind was emitting were muted. Nothing got through. His words were so...seductive. He pressed his forehead against mine, while his fingertip traced the bow of my lips and then slid slowly along my lower lip. I kissed his fingertip before he pulled his hand away. "What do I need?" The words came out playful.

"A man to hold you. A man to kiss you. You need me, Ivy. I can be exactly what you need."

Looking into his eyes, I stroked his cheek. His words washed over me slowly. The richness of his voice was irresistible. His lips were so close to mine. All I had to do was press my lips to his. Then we could be together. Then he could be my man. Man? The mental haze was fighting to maintain its hold. It was pressing further into my mind, but small thoughts slipped out. *Man.* He wasn't a man though. Then, what was he? I couldn't remember. *Bond.* The bond. Ah, I remembered that. It frightened and fascinated me. The bond created that feeling of oneness with Collin. Where was that now? Why couldn't I feel it? Didn't he lead me here?

It was as if he knew the power he held over me was fading. His voice sounded more demanding this time, "Kiss me, Ivy." He knotted his hands in my hair, but I didn't move. Where was the bond? The bond never went away. It would be there until one of us died. If this were Collin, I'd feel him. The bond would be telling me things.

Reaching out, I tried to brush his mind, *Collin. Say something to me. Speak to me the way that only you can.*

I waited but there was no reply. No bond. The boy laying on top of me wasn't Collin. He couldn't be. The fog that clouded my brain lifted. Suddenly I could think again. I could feel things besides lust. Anger surged through me. An imposter—the Lorren—had nearly trapped me here. I would have been a golden flower, trapped in this Godforsaken place forever! My jaw locked as rage spilled through my veins, flooding every part of me.

I spit in his face, "Get off of me. I know who you are." White-hot heat pooled in my fingertips. Collin sat up looking horrified.

"I can't let you leave. I have to hold you here…don't!" But I did. Whatever made my eyes rim and my hair turn to violet flames didn't agree with the Lorren. The false Collin fizzled like water on a hot skillet, and I was alone.

CHAPTER TWENTY-TWO

I felt totally drained after my encounter with the Lorren. It played me perfectly. If I'd been weaker, if my mind accepted the fake Collin easier, I'd be another decoration in the golden tomb. It made me question everything I saw. Things shouldn't be taken for granted down here. It was too dangerous. Maybe that wasn't even the exit. It was possible that the rust-colored light at the end of the tunnel wasn't even real, or if it was, it just a manifestation that the Lorren concocted to screw with me. Or maybe this screwed up maze was a circle, and was going to dump me out back at the beginning. I decided not to think about it. I'd have to deal with things as they came. At least I didn't have to worry about the Lorren attacking me again for a while. I had the feeling that it left, not that it was gone. It was unclear to me what had caused it to retreat. Rimming violet eyes and flaming hair never did anything before. I should have asked Eric if the Valefar made the Lorren, or if the Martis stuck it here. Then I'd have a better idea of how to kill it.

Brushing myself off, I stood and straightened my shirt, assessing myself. It seemed like I was okay. I just felt like an emotional train wreck. Things couldn't possibly get worse from this point. The Lorren almost cast me in gold, Eric and Shannon were lost or killed and turned into golden lilies, and I was alone again. Of course it would show me Collin. I knew it walking in, but it still messed with me horribly. Seeing him in front of me, even his likeness, was crushing. He was close. And I was getting closer. I just had to get out of this hole of gold and sapphires and find him. My hand glided over my waistband where the Guardian's tooth was concealed. The shard had torn a small hole in my black shirt. The deadly silver tip poked through the fabric. It needed to be covered. For all I knew, it could kill me. I already knew the tooth would kill Valefar and Martis. Since I was a combination of the two, this tooth was likely one of the only things that could kill me completely. I'd accidentally overheard Eric's discussion with Julia back when he was the Seeker, and it reminded me of what they'd said about me. For some reason my combined powers made me extra hard to kill. They had devised a way to permanently get rid of me. And I was standing in it. That seemed like an awfully big coincidence. If I hadn't been following the bond, I wouldn't have believed that was all it was.

Now, to cover the tip of the tooth. If I got sliced with Celestial Silver or Brimstone, I'd heal. But the sapphire serum inside was another story. The best thing to do was to cover it somehow. But, how? It's not like there was the Underworld Gift Shoppee where I could buy a holster. Glancing around, I looked down and watched the sapphires glittering under my feet. "No, it couldn't be that simple," I said to myself. Bending down, I used the tooth to pop up one of the smaller dark blue stones. I held the rock in the palm of my hand and rolled it around. Then, I pressed the shard's poisoned tip into the rock. It melted into the stone like it was putty. The sapphire was like a sparkly pen cap. I removed the blue stone from the tooth and looked at the silver tooth.

Did the poisoned tip touch the Lorren? Is that why I regained my powers? Did the sapphire serum in the tooth lessen the Lorren's mental hold on me? Something changed, allowing me to free myself, but I wasn't sure what. Intoxication doesn't even begin to describe what the Lorren did to me. Losing control over my body like that scared me. Lust had never burned inside me that way before. Whenever it popped up, I tried to squash it back down. The thought of being totally out of control with some guy didn't sound appealing, but back there—when I thought he was Collin—it sounded perfect.

"Stop thinking about it," I scolded myself. I slid the gemstone cover back onto the point of the Guardian's tooth, and put it away. The little stone pressed into me, but it wasn't so uncomfortable that I'd move the weapon. It needed to remain hidden. It might be the only thing I had that could kill Kreturus.

I started walking towards the light that was shining at the end of the tunnel. I couldn't see anything to confirm that it was the end of the tunnel, but I had to go look. If it was the beginning again, I don't know what I'd do. That was the worst thing I could imagine. I couldn't go through this again. At least having Eric and Shannon there for a while before helped. Now, I was on my own.

The golden flowers thinned as I walked. I promised myself right then and there that I wouldn't freak out no matter what was at the end of this tunnel. Falling apart wasn't an option. The pep talk I gave myself did absolutely nothing for what lay in wait at the end of the Lorren.

CHAPTER TWENTY-THREE

My feet pounded the golden floor as I ran toward him screaming his name. Eric's body was steaming with white vapors that drifted upward from open sores all over his body. He lay on his back, unmoving, less than three feet from the end of the Lorren. The exit was right in front of him. It was right in front of me.

"NO!" I screamed, as I crashed to the ground next to him. "Eric!" My arms wrapped around his body, and I pulled his head into my lap. Frantic fingers touched his face trying to assess the damage. There was so much. Sobs lodged in my throat. I couldn't breathe.

His golden eyes looked up at me. Recognition was slow. "Ivy," he breathed. "Don't touch me. Deadly." His back arched in pain as an ear piercing cry erupted from his throat. I didn't let go. I didn't back away completely horrified, although I was. His skin was melting, being eaten away by something I couldn't see. The worst parts were on his arms and chest. Sections of flesh were eaten away past the muscle, and down to the whites of his bone.

I held his face, trying to call him back to me. "Eric. Eric. Listen to me. What happened? Tell me what did this?" His flesh was burning away like a smoldering flame devouring a dried out leaf. The smell of burnt flesh filled the air.

Eric kept trying to speak, ignoring my question, "Don't. Put me down. It'll kill you."

Frantically, I asked, "What? What'll kill me? What did this?"

His face contorted with pain. His voice was changing, and becoming more garbled. The acid that was eating his flesh was inside his throat, destroying his voice. Killing him from within. "Brimstone. Dust. She…" he trailed off.

Brimstone?

Horror washed over my face. Brimstone was the only thing that could kill Martis. Eric's body was covered in it. But, the dust was so fine I couldn't even see it. Oh my God! He'd breathed it in, too! It was destroying him in every possible way at the same time. Tears welled up in my eyes. I knew the Brimstone wouldn't affect me. My demon blood protected me from it. Apryl's necklace had a Brimstone disc that constantly touched my skin. I was immune. Eric was not.

I hushed him, "It's all right. It won't hurt me. I'll stay with you. I won't leave you here like this." Tears rolled down my cheeks. I couldn't help it. Eric was my anchor. I didn't understand him very well, but he'd helped me more than words could say. And, now I was holding him in my lap while he died, helpless to do anything about it.

This was a slow death. The Brimstone spread over his body, sending out runners like mold and then growing into the flesh and dissolving it. When the Brimstone finished devouring the flesh, it ate down to the bone. His eyes closed after a while and he lay shuddering in pain in my lap. He kept trying to say something, but I couldn't understand him. The Brimstone dust had devoured his vocal cords.

His face was one of the only places the deadly dust had yet to spread. Eric's eyes pleaded with me, remaining locked on my face. His breaths were slight, but his golden eyes didn't waver. I spoke softly to him, "I'd do anything to stop this. Eric, I don't know what to do."

Well, that wasn't true. One thing crossed my mind. It was the only thing that would save him, but the cost was too high. I could give him a demon kiss and turn him Valefar. But, Eric would rather die. But looking into his eyes, I wasn't so certain any more. His body had gone still. Too many muscles were torn, dissolved away from bone for him to move. The pain was etched across his face as the microscopic spears of Brimstone dust shot blackened lines up his neck.

His eyes remained locked on my face, pleading. But pleading for what? What if he only wanted to tell me something? What if he wanted to die, but I turned him into a Valefar? It might not even work. I'd never given anyone a demon kiss. I didn't know if I could even make someone into a Valefar. My blood was tainted with angel blood. It might not work. Then what? What would he be then? Oh my God! There wasn't enough time, and his eyes! The pain, the remorse, the pleading! Maybe he wanted me to.

I asked, "You want me to, don't you? Eric, I can't do it. I'm not a full Valefar. It may not even work." I knew he was running out of time. He blinked slowly at me. His eye lids were so heavy that he couldn't keep them open. He was slipping away. His life was about to end in failure. The things he'd told me about the night Lydia died and how he failed her rushed to the front of my mind. He was leaving behind a legacy of failure, his own kind thought he was a traitor, and he died in Hell following the girl that he was trying to help. Me! No, this can't happen. He couldn't die. This was my fault! He wouldn't have been labeled a traitor if it weren't for me. I didn't know what to do. Eric blinked one final time, and did not reopen his eyes. The shallow pants that filled his chest ceased and his body lay utterly still.

"Awh, shit. Eric!" Panic shot through my trembling arms. There was no other choice. Let him die, or kiss him. Decide! I pressed my eyes closed and leaned in, hoping this was what he wanted. My lips connected with Eric's. There was no time to be gentle. I'd waited too long. I should have asked him while he could speak. But, that look on his face was telling me he didn't want to die. He didn't want to leave yet. There was a way to keep him alive, but he'd hate me for it.

Especially if I misunderstood the plea on his face.

I kissed him fiercely, pressing his lips to mine. When my tongue darted between his lips I could taste the sulfuric residue from the Brimstone in his mouth. I didn't stop. Something inside me awakened. Something dark and powerful. I wanted him. It burned inside of me like nothing I'd ever known. I deepened the kiss until I felt it, something warm and light—his soul. I didn't need souls to maintain my strength the way Valefar did. I didn't need to devour humans to stay alive. I didn't need to trap and kill Martis to survive, but here I was destroying the little life that remained in Eric.

His soul slid free and floated into my mouth. I nearly choked on how smooth and sweet it tasted. All of Eric's essence, his entire spirit was gone. I held a limp body in my arms. Dropping him quickly, I sliced the flesh across his Martis mark with my comb, and then ripped open my thumb. Blood flowed from my wound. I squeezed my thumb, getting as much blood as I could to fill the scar I'd placed on Eric's forehead. The marred skin greedily absorbed the scarlet liquid, wanting more than I'd given. I cut my palm wide open, and held it to his face. His wound soaked it in quickly. When I took my palm away, Eric lay still, neither moving or breathing. I spoke nonsense to him softly, telling him everything would be all right. Maybe it was more to myself. This had to work. It had to. I could do other Valefar things. I half hoped he would sit up and smile at me. But if he did, he'd want to kill me. To save his life, I'd made him the very thing he despised.

The black veins of Brimstone stopped spreading through his skin, though I didn't notice when. When he still didn't move I cut every finger on my hand, and sliced my palm open several times, trying to get enough blood into his cut, but he hadn't moved. Eric remained utterly still, deathly still. Tears welled up in my eyes and I buried my face in his chest.

It didn't work.

Damn it! Tears streaked my face in silent sobs. My fingers remained locked on his shirt. I couldn't let go. The Lorren won. It got him. Eric would become one of the golden flowers on the walls of this fucking tomb!

Anger coursed through me. Everyone was going to die, because of me. I released Eric's shirt and backed away from his lifeless body. Valefar desires coursed through me. Dark magic burned deep within me. Part of me was horrified to learn that I enjoyed tasting his soul. I shoved down those feelings as far as they would go and screamed. The scream echoed through the Lorren and bounced back in my face. I took one last look at Eric and turned away.

I walked out of the Lorren alone that day feeling utterly destroyed. I'd expected the Lorren to tempt me with the one thing I wanted but didn't have—Collin. Instead it showed me the one thing I didn't need, but couldn't resist—the soul of a good man.

CHAPTER TWENTY-FOUR

"How could you!" Shannon's shrieking voice broke the depressed mental haze looming over me. I flinched at the sound of her voice. When I left the Lorren, there was no trace of her. I continued following the bond, descending deeper and deeper into the Underworld. Time passed in an unreal way after I left Eric. I didn't know how long I'd been walking. I assumed Shannon was dead, too. I thought I'd never see her again. The sound of her voice surprised me. Turning slowly, I couldn't believe it was her, but it was. And she was pissed. Her shoulder collided with my chest and sent me hurling to the ground. Her rage shocked me out of my stupor. Did she think that I killed Eric?

"Shannon, get off of me!" I yelled. She pinned me to the cave floor, thrusting her dagger at my neck. Confusion slid across my face as I blocked and threw her off of me. She was trying to kill me! There was no hesitation in her swing, and rage was plastered all over her face. Quickly, I jumped to my feet and we circled each other slowly, like two tigers ready to rip each other apart.

Shannon's emerald eyes were wild. "I told you. I told you! Once you changed and became one of them that I would have no choice. I'd kill you. And out of all people to demon kiss, you kiss Eric!" Her fist collided with my cheek and it felt as if my face exploded. I twisted out of her grip before her blade could cut me. Just because Celestial Silver hadn't killed me in the past, I wasn't taking any chances now. Somehow I doubted I'd survive if she plunged her blade into my heart.

She ranted hysterically, screaming at me. "I should have ended this sooner! There is no way for a prophecy to remain unfulfilled. You're evil, Ivy! Eric couldn't see it, but I could! I kept telling him that you'd changed. That you were evil now. To end it. To end you! And he defended you! YOU!"

Anger coursed through me. What was she was saying? She already wrote me off! I probably should have reached for my comb, but I didn't. I was too irate. "When, Shannon? When did you think I turned evil? Was it before we came down here, when we flew from New York, or was it before that?"

"It doesn't matter when! I was right! Evil doesn't even begin to describe you!" She jumped toward me, and her blade pierced my skin leaving a red trail in its wake.

"Shannon, you're insane! Stop it! I didn't kill him! It was someone else! Shan, please!" Something felt so wrong, like I was missing a huge puzzle piece, but I couldn't figure out what it was. I was too busy trying to keep her dagger from plunging into my heart. She was going to kill me if I didn't fight back, but I couldn't. The punches I threw were halfhearted. I wanted her to stop and see me for what I am, but she didn't. "SHANNON! STOP!"

"NO!" Her face was deep red. Every muscle in her body was tensed, ready to strike. We were circling one another again. Panting, she bellowed at me, "I can't believe we were friends! I can't believe I protected you. You! The freak abomination Hell-child. I should have known what you were! You were such a slut, and what you did with Collin. You saved the enemy! And Eric just stood there. You killed him that night... and you can die tonight!"

The silver blade flashed as she found an opening. Enraged, she launched her blade directly at my heart. Something inside me snapped. I felt it crack open and spill. Power broke free and flowed through my hands in rushing fury. Heat burned my fingers like I'd lit them on fire, but that wasn't the part that shocked me. Each fingertip burned with a bright violet flame and a pure white center. The flames rushed at Shannon, engulfing her in light. She screamed, and was absorbed by the flames.

CHAPTER TWENTY-FIVE

I wanted to die. Tears streamed down my face blurring my vision. My feet fumbled as I tried to keep walking, but I couldn't. I knew Shannon and I weren't friends the way we had been. The past was the past. We were best friends since we were born. During that time we were inseparable. But lately she was different. She was more Martis than anything else. She chose them over me. Seventeen years of friendship was destroyed in a couple of seconds—the second Jake kissed me, the second Collin saved me. But her hatred wasn't something that just happened. It had been going on for a while. Like last year, when I thought she'd helped me with without judgment when I flamed out after I thought my sister died. Apparently that wasn't the case. Her condemnation stung. I wiped the tears out of my eyes and sat down. The sound of distant demon birds filled the air. I'd move when the grackles got closer.

Crying does nothing, but for some reason the tears didn't stop. Maybe it was because she was right. I was evil, and I was crying for myself and not Shannon. I shouldn't have kissed Eric. I shouldn't have left him in the Lorren. But I did. And Shannon. My God, what did I do to Shannon? When I fought the Guardian, I felt power surge through me, but this was different. It felt like light and darkness combined and did something to her. She wasn't dead. Her heart was beating while the flashes of light did whatever they did. After the light dimmed there was an afterglow—a black mirror. I pressed on its hot surface. It was made of the same squishy stuff as the last one I'd seen, but this time I saw Shannon on the other side. She was lying on the floor surrounded by pews at St. Bart's. I backed away from the mirror, and it shattered. The black pieces fell to the ground and vanished. No, I didn't kill Shannon. I sent her home, but I had no idea how. My powers were out of control. I didn't know what they did or how I called them. Were they Martis or Valefar? Or something worse? Something that only the Prophecy One could do?

I slumped forward, resting my head on my knees. I'd undertaken the impossible task of trying to rescue Collin from the pits of Hell. What made me think I could do this? Love. The answer popped up in my mind instantly. I thought I could save him because of true love? It sounded idiotic, but it was true. After all, what was the difference between what I was doing and going back into enemy territory for a fallen ally? None. There was no difference, and I was on my own. There was no one to catch me when I fell. I was utterly alone, and I would be alone for the rest of the time I was down here. It made me wonder, how far would I go to save the people I loved? Instant bravery didn't pour from me when I needed it. It felt more like I was flying by the seat of my pants and they were ripping. When the Guardian went after Apryl I thought it would rip her to shreds. I fought that monster because I had to. My mission sounded insane, but my world was insane. I was at the center of an ancient prophecy. Everyone wanted a piece of me.

The rustling of the dragon's wings passed high above me. Good. As long as that thing was nearby the grackles would leave me alone. Perhaps sitting still wasn't wise, but I wasn't moving for the time being. I needed a plan. It was impossible to tell when my powers would surge. That made them very unpredictable. I was going to need another way to deal with the demons, Valefar, and Kreturus when the time came.

The demons and Valefar were down here although I hadn't seen any yet. But I knew they were here. I'd seen them in several visions. The demons and select Valefar surrounded a place that looked like black stone from the outside and a palace from within. It wasn't surrounded with pretty landscaping, but quite the opposite. The land was almost sickly looking—torn and bled dry. It rose high on spikes as far as the eye could see. It wasn't smooth rust colored stone like here. The ground was barren, hard, and black. Nothing grew. There was no light. The place was drenched in darkness. I was certain I would see that place before I left the Underworld.

A plan. What kind of plan could I devise? I couldn't just run in, all samurai warrior on them, and try to slash everything with my silver blade. There would be too many of them. That meant I had to sneak in. I was back to relying on stealth to get me inside. I sucked at stealth, but it seemed to be my only option. I was still going to have to sneak in and plan to efanotate Collin out. If something went wrong, I had no back-up plan. I'd be trapped here forever. Kreturus wanted me as his bride. Whatever that meant. Since a demon kiss was horrid, I assumed a demon marriage was fantastically terrifying.

Stretching, I arched my back and leaned against the wall. Gazing into the sky, I looked around for the dragon, but the cavern ceiling was an inky black. The dragon blended in so well that it was invisible. What role did that beast play in all of this? Was it watching me and reporting to someone? Or was the dragon wild? I'd assumed everything down here was Kreturus'. But, maybe that wasn't true. I couldn't imagine anyone taming that gigantic creature enough to make it obey. Startled, I flinched when I saw the dragon's glowing red eyes in the shadows across from me.

I didn't know if it could understand me, but I spoke to it anyway, "Who are you? Why are you following me?" I didn't expect it to answer. It was an animal. But at the same time, I felt like it understood me. It's ancient eyes held wisdom that I lacked. What kind of wisdom they contained was beyond me.

I rose, slowly, and walked towards it. Its enormous head rested on its forearms. The creature's talons were retracted. It watched me as I crossed into the shadows where it lay without moving. I stopped without getting too close. "What do you want with me? That must be the reason you're following me. Everyone wants me. Am I your next meal or are you looking for something else?" I cocked my head, looking at the beast. It was beautiful. I'm sure that made me a total freak—admiring the beauty of something sent to kill me—but he was. Each massive scale was black in the center that faded into a rich purple at the edge. When the light moved across his body, it illuminated him in a breathtaking way. His eyes were brilliantly stunning and utterly terrifying. Those jeweled eyes followed me, seeming to understand what I said, though he didn't respond. Before I turned away I said, "You're the most beautiful thing I've ever seen...Everything from your eyes to your lacey wings. I know I should be terrified of you, but I'm not." We looked at each other, surrounded by silence.

Eventually, I backed away and began walking again. After a few minutes, a gust of wind hit my back, as the dragon took off and flew away. Maybe he wasn't smart. Maybe he couldn't speak. I didn't care. He seemed like me in some ways—massively powerful and completely alone.

CHAPTER TWENTY-SIX

Descending deeper into Hell was terrifying. There were more beasts down here. They had grotesque bodies and deformed heads. Most of them looked like rotting beasts that were dipped in acid with decaying skin falling off their gangly frames. And the stench! The sulfur was so thick I could barely breathe. The living weren't supposed to enter down here, but I was very much alive. The oxygen could run out. That was a thought I didn't even want to ponder. I moved my body silently through the shadows, avoiding any creature I saw. It made my progress slow down significantly, but I couldn't risk being caught.

During the last descent, before I found all the freak-show creatures, I practiced calling my powers. I tried to call the purple flames that engulfed Shannon, or the shattering fists that cracked the Guardian's teeth. Fixating on anger didn't work although I did notice I was usually pissed when my powers came to me. The powers had to be a mixture of good and bod, although they felt neither Martis or Valefar. If they'd been Valefar, I'd know. All of their power is paid for in pain. Using the power when it came to me didn't hurt. It actually felt good. That's how I knew it wasn't Martis power either. They didn't reward their goodie-two shoed servants. It was something else. It was me. If I called tooth-cracking power once, I should be able to call it again. If I threw Shannon's ass back to Long Island on a violet bolt of lightning, I should be able to do it again. But no matter how hard I tried, nothing happened. My eyes didn't even rim. Maybe my powers only came when I needed them. I hoped to God I was right, because there was nothing to protect me down here. My silver comb couldn't ward off an army of demons. I was in their land now and they were all around me.

Pushing my back into the shadows, I edged around a stalactite, as two demons passed on the other side. Their voices gurgled as they walked by, "…said he knows that her powers are immature." I pressed my back to the stone, trying not to breathe. They were talking about me? Immature powers sounded right. That would explain why I couldn't control them.

Another raspy demon voice answered, "Does not matter. He will show her how to use them. She is most precious to him. Master is patient. He will wait for his bride."

My heart pounded in my chest. I listened as they walked away, but they said nothing else about me. I closed my eyes slowly and rested my head against the stone behind my back. "He knows I'm here." Breathing deeply, I tried to deal with that information. Before I could guess that Kreturus thought I might be here, but now, I knew for certain that he was aware of my presence.

A rock skittered across the ground and slid into the side of my foot. Instantly, I jumped backwards and scanned the darkness. There were very few paths in this part of the Underworld. The stone floor was jagged and dropped off constantly. It made it difficult to sneak around in the shadows. I might fall into a chasm at any moment. But, that also meant that no one else should be in the shadows, not unless they could fly. So who was watching me?

My eyes fixated on a dark patch certain that something was there. But, I saw nothing. My Martis vision couldn't cut through some of the shadows. It was like the inky blackness was a being, rather than the absence of light. The thick, dark masses oozed, filling every crack and crevice. I stayed away from those, too. Right then the weird shadows were the only things dangerous that I saw. Were the shadow creatures throwing rocks at me? I shook my head at thinking something so stupid, and turned to continue my slow progress through the pointed stones.

I didn't get very far. Suddenly, a hand was at my throat, and I slammed backwards into the rock. A shallow gasp left my body, as the air was smacked out of me. I grabbed at the hand, trying to pry the fingers loose, before looking up into red rimmed eyes. Fear shot through me in an icy blast.

"Oh my God. Eric."

Every muscle in his body was flexed, pressing me into the stone. He breathed in my ear, crushing his face to mine. His voice came out fast and hushed, "What? Don't like what you did? Is that why you ran away and left me for the Lorren, Ivy?" I tried to push him away, but he tightened his grip. His fingers pressed harder against my throat cutting off my air supply. Panic spread through my body. Wide eyed I looked at him, unable to speak. His eyes were rimmed in red. The bloodlust of battle was making him act like this. If his eyes pooled red, if the gold completely disappeared, then that meant he'd totally lost control. Death by Valefar wasn't something I wanted. Jake's attack, the bastard who gave me the demon kiss and turned me into the freak show I am, still terrified me. The Lorren and the Guardian were different. I could fight those. I wasn't able to fight Jake. I would have happily kicked his ass, but he'd trapped me before I knew what was happening. Later, I learned from Collin that a Valefar consumed by lust wanted nothing more than to capture his prey. Right now that was me. Eric was singularly focused on me. *Don't fight him* I thought to myself. *Try and talk him down, wait for his eyes to return to amber.*

I rasped, "Eric. I thought you were dead." I twisted sharply and slipped out of his grip.

"I was," he said, advancing again with his muscles flexed. "And you left me. Being turned Valefar kind of knocked me on my ass. At the very least, I thought you'd wait around for me to wake up." Each step he took towards me made my heart beat faster. The insane look in his eyes revealed an Eric that I didn't know. It was like someone turned him inside out, and the only thing that was left was the hatred, betrayal, and pain. It was raw and flowing off him in waves.

"Eric," I said with my hands up in front of me, trying to back away. "I didn't know. I tried to save you. You couldn't speak. I thought this was what you wanted. I thought…"

His face pinched together in a scowl and he cut me off, "You fucking thought wrong." I flinched at his words. He leaned in so close to me that we were nearly touching, "Don't like what you made, Ivy? Too fucking bad. Deal with it! And since you forgot to bind me, there's nothing to protect you from me."

My heart was racing. This wasn't the Eric I knew. Apryl still had some Aprylness to her, but Eric—he was gone. This was a Valefar! What did I do? Oh God. He didn't want me to turn him. There was no way to take that back. Stay focused. Calm him down or kill him. There were no other options. And Eric was getting madder. I needed him to talk, to get rid of the anger. Unsure of what to say, I said whatever popped into my mind, "I didn't need to bind you."

He tensed, breathing heavily in front of me, hesitating. "Yes, you did. I remember every last speck of pain you caused me. I remember the dust and then that kiss stripping my soul from my body. I'm going to crack you into tiny pieces right here. Half of Hell is looking for you to drag back to the old demon. The other half wants you for themselves. But, I want you dead. I'll drain you the way you did me and leave you in the Lorren to die!" He lunged at me, slamming me into the wall. I took the hit, not fighting back. But, I couldn't let him think I was the one who killed him. Whoever did that was gone by the time I got there.

"Do it!" I screamed in his face, leaning towards him. "Do it, Eric. Kiss me. Rip me apart. Ravage me." He hesitated. I knew his memories were blurred. He confused the brimstone dust with his demon kiss. I needed rational Eric, and I knew he was still in there. He had to be. I smacked my open palms into his chest and screamed, "Do it!" His hand gripped the back of my neck hard, and jerked me towards him. His lips were right in front of mine. His hard breaths washed across my mouth. I didn't fight. I didn't pull away. Confusion lined his face, and he hesitated. "Do it," I growled. His grip on my neck became tighter, as he pulled me roughly to him. I stared at his eyes, hoping they would return to normal.

They didn't. He pressed his lips to my cheek hard and breathed in my ear. A shiver ran down my spine. I tried to suppress it, but I flinched. A wolf-like smile formed slowly on his lips. "Ivy, you're all smoke and mirrors. All bravado and no bite. Your heart is pounding beneath your breast in that thin little shirt. It's beating so hard and fast that it's going to explode." He grazed his teeth along my neck, pressed his face into my soft skin, and inhaled deeply. "You're delicious, Ivy. Absolutely mouthwatering..."

I stiffened. "Do it, Eric. What are you waiting for? Every Valefar wants to kill their maker. I made you. DO IT!" The vein in my neck was throbbing as I yelled. He was right. I was all smoke and mirrors. And this wasn't working.

Eric pressed his lips against my cheek, dragging them across my skin, inhaling my scent deeply. He stopped at the corner of my mouth, and turned slightly to rest his forehead against mine. The viselike hold he had on the back of my neck softened. His voice was a whisper, "Why didn't you bind me?"

"You were a warrior," I said softly. "warriors shouldn't be bound."

"I *am* a warrior. From the time I woke up, I fought. I've tracked you, following the scent of your blood. That is supposed to help a Valefar find their maker when they're called. I used it to track you. I killed the creatures that wanted you. You're mine, I told them. You're mine…" his voice trailed off and he looked up at me. His eyes weren't rimmed anymore. They were golden orbs.

I put my hand on his cheek, but he pushed it down and stepped away from me. "Eric, who covered you in Brimstone? Was it the Lorren?"

He arched an eyebrow at me, and turned his back. His hands slid together smoothly as he folded his arms. "It was you."

He spun around, anger painted across his face. "Eric, the Lorren was killing me while that happened to you. You were a few feet in front of me, right in front of the exit. I found you as I was leaving. Do you remember? I held you…I told you it would be all right, but it wasn't. You died in my arms. The entire time it looked like you were pleading with me, asking me to make it stop. This was the only way I knew to stop the pain. I turned you Valefar, but someone else covered you in brimstone dust first."

He stared at me, completely still. "But, I saw you. Shannon and I were ripped away from you and thrown out of the Lorren. I wanted to go back in…Shannon said no. She said to leave you. We fought and I walked away from her. I went back into the Lorren myself.

Within three steps, you appeared. I was so relieved. I figured that wind must have carried you through the Lorren as well. I spoke to you, but you didn't answer. When I approached to see if you were all right, you threw Brimstone dust on me. I was shocked, and inhaled more than I would have if anyone else had done it. I remember you disappearing, leaving me there to die, only to let me writhe and then turn me into a fucking Valefar! It was you! It was you."

"It was the Lorren. It doused you in the dust, not me. I swear to you. After the wind separated us, I walked through it on my own. It wasn't a tunnel. It was a maze. The Lorren almost killed me. Right before I found you, it looked like Collin. The mental fog it threw over me was so thick that I couldn't think. It wasn't a matter of *keep walking* like we'd thought going in. The Lorren didn't let me walk."

"Mental fog? There was no mental fog." He was quiet for a minute. "I remember everything, and it was you. Without this," he pointed at my pendant. His face pinched in confusion.

"I never take this off," my hand was over Apryl's necklace. "The Lorren would have appeared with it. No, it wasn't the Lorren. You're right. It was someone else. But the only other person was…"

Eric's face contorted with rage. "Shannon."

CHAPTER TWENTY-SEVEN

"Shit," Eric said, "They made her the Seeker! The Martis made her the Seeker and sent her after us. That's why she knew about the Lorren!" He turned and punched the cave wall. It cracked under his fist. The night of Eric's hearing was so chaotic that the memories blurred together. Shannon found us just as we were entering the portal to the Underworld. Casey ratted out my location. She'd seen the page I was reading in the archives. This entire time Shannon was waiting to ambush me. The bond leading us into the Lorren worked right into her plan. She killed Eric and tried to kill me! "Where is she?" Eric growled. His eyes were rimming.

My face contorted into a sneer as anger burned inside of me. I looked him straight in the eye and lied.

"I sent her back to Rome." Eric stared back, neither of us breaking the intense gaze.

Suddenly, Eric turned and tore off like a wild animal. He skidded to a stop, looked over his shoulder, and said, "I'm not done with you." Then he efanotated, and I was alone. His Valefar powers were already in full force. He didn't have to learn how to use them like I did, because I made him completely Valefar. That was how he snuck up on me this time, and it would mean he could do it again.

I screamed in an incoherent fury as my fists balled and I struck a stalactite, shattering it into a million tiny pieces. Why did I take so long to learn? I was so stupid! Shannon was trying to kill me. It made sense that she'd try to kill Eric too. He was a traitor as far as she was concerned. Fucking Martis. They thought everything was black and white. There was no middle ground. Shannon sided with them, choosing the Martis over me a long time ago. Anger coursed through me as every muscle in my body flexed, looking for something else to punch. It messed horribly with my head when she came after me, but I didn't see the point in killing Eric. He was trapped down here anyway. It's not like the Martis would have ever welcomed him back. But, he would have helped me. And now he was a deranged demon. The boy I knew was gone. My fist collided with another rock smashing it to bits.

CHAPTER TWENTY-EIGHT

The memory of my vision smashed into me with icy accuracy. I remembered the darkness, the slant of the cave floor, and the slick stone under my feet. My fingers grazed the cavern walls as I walked, dragging slowly over the cold stone. Hysteria rose in my throat, but I couldn't stop. Knowing what was ahead made my heart pound in my chest. With each step I took, the familiarity of it made me think I was one step closer to death. But, my visions weren't set-in-stone predications. It was possible that something else would happen—I just had no idea what.

When the glowing red ring of light appeared in the distance, my heart caught in my throat. Collin would come into view in a minute. His body would be ravaged, torn to shreds by demon talons, as he lay unconscious on the ground. Tears stung behind my eyes, but I couldn't let them fall. I rubbed my face hard, and took a deep breath. This was it. This is where I failed or succeeded. He needed me, and I needed him. He was my soul mate, and I wouldn't leave him here.

Lying on my stomach, I peered over the edge of the chasm. The gorge dropped off steeply and appeared to go on forever. A faint red glow emanated from somewhere deeper down in the ravine. Swallowing hard, I pushed my head back from the edge and looked up. Collin was in front of me. It was like my vision, which meant I would be spotted by demons at any moment. As soon as I thought it, the rest of the vision played out exactly as I'd seen it. Something tugged the shadows that masked my scent, and it didn't matter how hard I tried to retain them, the shadows were ripped away in one painful pull. As the last cold shadow was torn away, the demons caught my scent and turned their snarling deformed heads toward me—and charged.

The demons terrified me more than I could have imagined. Their vicious eyes focused on me, before the demons' bent and blackened bodies sprang into action. They moved like a wave as each one fought to reach me first. Glistening black scaly flesh had a red cast as they neared the edge of the ravine. Teeth like daggers, stained with blood, bore at me.

I efanotated to where Collin lie, with my scream cut off as my body seared from within. The scalding heat filled my body and when I thought I couldn't bare the pain for another moment, I was kneeling in front of Collin. A smug smile began to spread across my face. As I reached for Collin's hand to take him away with me, I saw the confusion unfold en masse as the demons tried to locate me. Within a matter of seconds, they saw that I'd reached my target.

I focused on the ruby ring to generate enough power to efanotate Collin and I to safety. Breathing hard, my finger trembled as I rubbed the stone. The heat began to lick my stomach and travel up my throat. Any second and we would be safe. The heat just had to intensify and surge through Collin, but there wasn't enough time. The enormous black wings appeared above us, descending like a falling plane. I held onto the heat, refusing to release the power of the only thing that could save us. The creature's black belly dropped out of the sky faster than I thought possible. That damn dragon had been following me the entire time I was down here. Why did he wait so long to kill me? Why allow me to get so close to Collin and then attack? A panicked cry flew from my throat. The monster's maw was wide open as it descended, making a horrific noise as it extended its taloned paws towards us. The massive blades came crashing down around us, pinning me to the ground. The creature shrieked, as it closed its gnarled fingers around Collin's limp body and pulled him away from me.

Cowering, screams continued to erupt from my throat. Only when it spread its wings and pushed upward, did I realize that it hadn't killed us. Collin's hand was pulled out of my grip as he ascended with the beast into blackness. I jumped to my feet shaking, screaming incoherent words at the dragon. Tears streamed down my cheeks and every blood vessel in my neck felt like it was on the verge of exploding. I was screaming incoherently, telling it to come back, taunting it.

The demons didn't attack. They stood motionless, watching my fit of rage.

Screams of pure hate flew from my mouth, as my throat was ripped raw by the sound. "WHERE ARE YOU?" I screamed at Kreturus. I knew he was here. My jaw locked as my nails bit into the flesh of my palm. "Come out you coward! It's me you want! I'm here and I'm not leaving!" I bellowed. My voice bounced off the cavern walls as the demons watched.

I stared at the darkness surrounding me with my jaw clenched tight. My heart was hammering in my ears, as I turned slowly. The place directly behind me, the darkness I'd crossed when I efanotated to Collin on the stone island—it moved. Complete certainty washed over me. It was Kreturus. I stepped towards the edge of the chasm.

"What did you do with him?" I growled.

A smooth, disembodied masculine voice flowed back at me, "He's mine, Ivy. You can't just take things that don't belong to you." The voice radiated through the blackness.

My sneer intensified, "He doesn't belong to you! You stole his life and trapped him in this one. I freed him. He is no longer Valefar. He does not belong to you." My eyes were transfixed on the darkness. I looked for the enormous red glowing coals there were his eyes the last time I'd seen him. I waited for the rancid breath to wash over me as he approached, but he stayed masked by the shadows on the other side of the ravine. A noise caused me to look above the black void. The dragon nestled its gauzy black wings tightly at its sides and sat as a sentry high above us. Collin was not in sight.

The voice answered, "That's where you are wrong. Everything in this realm is mine. If the darkness can touch it, it belongs to me. Nothing is beyond my reach. Not your love. Not your sister… No one."

Apryl appeared out of the darkness and remained perfectly still. Her cheeks were streaked with tearstains. She was frozen in a silent scream with terror etched across her face.

Alone in the blackness, surrounded by demons, I felt the rage festering in every inch of my body. My eyes burned, as I breathed, instantly pooling violet. My jaw locked and I said nothing. Apryl's words from the Pool of Lost Souls echoed through my mind, *Kill Kreturus!* But how? How! "What do you want?"

"What I've always wanted." The voice was smooth and seemed closer. I turned expecting to see the massive demon looming over my shoulder, but no one was there. He spoke into my opposite ear and I flinched. "You."

Faltering, I took a step back. "I'm not for sale." My voice lost its fury, but none of the venom.

"What if I offered you something that you already want? What if you came willingly?" His voice spoke from within the shadows across from me on my side of the pit. There was a faint outline where he stood in the darkness.

"I'd rather die." I spit the words at him with hatred. He was toying with me, but his words were difficult to ignore. It was impossible to maintain my rage. Frozen, I stood there. Listening.

"You don't want to free your sister?" he cooed. "You wouldn't restore her soul if it was within your power? You wouldn't give her back her life?" he asked.

I didn't answer. How could I? He continued, "I don't think we want different things. I think you would be secure in knowing that you and your sister were safe. Control over your fate would be within your reach. No more prophecies to bend to. No more commands to follow. No reason to prove yourself to anyone. You'd have complete control over your life..."

Anger surged through me. His words were playing me, and I could feel my resolve swaying. That pissed me off. Ignoring everything he'd said, I yelled, "Show yourself, you coward! You keep hiding behind shadows, too afraid to show your ugly face. But you forget, I've already seen you. I've already snuck in here and saw your evil form. Stop trying to manipulate me. I won't bend. There is no way in Hell that I'd ever help you."

He laughed, "I'm only offering you what you already want. And the form you saw before was the illusion. It was your own making, Ivy. You imagined the heinous demon that could pull you into Hell and make you his slave. You created that reality, including what I looked like. In reality, I have no form. No shape. No body. I am power, a force of pure destruction, and utter devastation. The Martis trapped me here, but they made an oversight." My heart sank. Shit. Al was right. He did find a way around it. Kreturus laughed, "You already know, don't you? I've not been stuck in this prison for some time. If I enter another form, our powers combine and I am free. You wouldn't lose your free will Ivy. You would just be more powerful. Powerful enough to restore life to the only family member you have left."

It felt like ice slid down my spine. I could barely breathe. His words seduced me, offering everything and requiring nothing of me, but to allow him use of my body. I stared into the blackness, revolted by how easily he could tempt me. Words fell out of my mouth and I knew they were right without contemplating. "No. If you want me, you'll have to kill me first. And I'm done with this conversation." I turned on my heel ready to walk away. I had no idea where I was going, I only knew I had to find Collin and get away from Kreturus. I felt my will weakening. The more he spoke, the more his words sounded logical. I had to remind myself that if he had my cooperation, he would open the gates of Hell. Demons and the other evil spawn I saw walking around would overflow from the Underworld and destroy my world. Kreturus needed it as a stepping-stone to overtake the angels realm. Earth was middle ground, a neutral zone. No, I couldn't let him win. But, I couldn't kill him. As he said, he was pure power, a trapped force with no physical body to destroy. Why did I think I could kill him? Why did I ever think this would be easy?

His voice spoke softly behind me, "You cannot walk away from me, Ivy Taylor."

"Then stop me," I blurted out. But, I'd underestimated his ability. I thought if he had no form, his powers would be hindered, but they weren't. Suddenly, I felt like I was in a straightjacket and slammed into an invisible wall. My feet were heavy and glued to the floor.

"Ivy," he sounded amused, "this is petty. Of course I can stop you. Of course I could end your fragile life and snap you in two. I can do anything I want to you, and you can't stop me. But, that isn't my desire. I don't want you that way. I want you to invite me—willingly. This is your last chance. Don't refuse me."

His invisible bindings dropped and I turned, staring into the darkness. "Or what?" I screamed. "You've taken everything from me. There is nothing— NOTHING—else you can do that would make me willingly offer you anything." I spat the words like they were poison. Hate fueled my passion, and his amusement fanned the flames. Kreturus' hollow laugh reverberated off the cavern walls. His demons drew away, cowering. The dragon, high on the cliff, buried its head under its wing after giving me a look that said it thought I was an idiot. I sensed the same thing they did. His power was so thick I could feel it sliding over my skin. Shivering I backed away.

I came down here and I lost. I saved no one, but I'd be damned if I was going to let him take me. There was no way that thing was welcome in my body. As Kreturus' power ebbed, the darkness thickened. Things happened too quickly to think. The swirling black mass in front of me flowed outward like a storm cloud bursting open. Stunned, I watched as it swirled around creating a space in the middle. In that space, I could make out a prone form lying still on the ground. My heart sank. *No, no, no!* My gaze jerked up towards the dragon's perch, but he was gone.

Shaking I ran straight towards the black mass screaming. But, when I threw myself against the wall of darkness, I was launched back. My body flew through the air and collided with a stalactite before sliding to the floor. Pain shot through me on impact, but it didn't stop me. As I righted myself, rage engulfed me. I felt the instant transformation consume me. My eyes pooled instantly. Violet tongues of fire raced down each strand of hair until the tips of my long curls glowed bright purple. It was like flipping a switch. There was no fear. Only intense anger.

Rage.

Eric had said to contain my rage when this happened last time. My inability to mask my emotions cost me the Martis' trust. And it later cost Eric his life. And now, there was nothing left to lose. Strength flooded my body as Kreturus' voice resonated in a hideous laugh throughout the cavern.

Suddenly, the black cloud became translucent and shone like oil on blacktop. Its spinning shifted directions as the blacked mist streamed rapidly towards the prone boy who was trapped in the center of the vortex—Collin. The oily mass flowed rapidly into the sliced skin that covered his body. Collin remained inert, but his body stiffened and writhed as the black mass slid into him through his marred flesh.

Again, I ran towards him, trying to penetrate the black mist that was surrounded Collin. But, the invisible force that surrounded him threw me backwards, screaming. As I jumped to my feet to try and reach Collin another way the sound of wind rushing through the cavern whistled at a deafening pitch, and paralyzed me. My hands instinctively covered my ears to block out the noise. I looked up and saw Collin's body within the vortex, spine arched, hovering above the ground. The last of the inky darkness was sucked into his wounds, and his limp body dropped to the floor. Everything began to pass in a matter of seconds that felt like eternity.

Complete coldness engulfed me, filling the pit of my stomach like lead. I didn't need an instruction manual to know what had happened. The black powerful mass that spoke to me, the thing that was Kreturus, the thing that wanted to reside inside of me—it was inside of Collin.

Kreturus wanted to control me and use my powers. When I refused, he chose the one person I couldn't deny. The boy who held my heart. My soul mate.

Collin.

We were now enemies again and it was so much worse than before. Before the stake was his life or mine. But now, it was kill him or let Kreturus destroy the world. The demon had to be vulnerable in this form. Kreturus inhabited Collin's body, and that body had limitations. This was my only chance.

Shaking, I walked towards Collin's prone form. My fingers felt for the cold silver of the Guardian's tooth that was tucked in my waistband. It was the most powerful weapon I had. That tooth was the only thing that could destroy a person who had both Valefar blood and Martis blood flowing through their veins. If I killed Collin, Kreturus might die with him. I'd destroy the old demon and wouldn't unleash evil upon the world. It would end the battle, and I would not become the girl in the prophecy.

Slowly I approached Collin, hesitating. I wanted Kreturus dead. He was responsible for killing my mother and turning my sister into a Valefar. He stole Collin from me in a way that wouldn't allow me to ever get him back. My Collin was gone. When he awoke he would be crazier than Eric. The massive powers of the demon that inhabited his body would dominate him.

Kreturus had no compassion. He ended lives without thought, bringing pain and misery upon anyone he chose. Now the form delivering that hideous evil was the boy I loved.

I didn't want to do this. Collin saved me. He loved me. But that boy wasn't Collin anymore. Kreturus stole him from me, and in a cruel twist of fate, I'd have to kill the only boy I'd ever loved.

Certainty washed over me as I stared at Collin's sleeping form—I couldn't survive this. There was no way to plunge the Guardian's tooth into Collin's heart and live with myself. I didn't care that Kreturus was in there. He still looked like Collin. It was still Collin's body lying in front of me. Dropping to my knees, I sat next to his motionless body. His perfect face was caught between the worlds of sleep and wake. There was no time to think; no time to know if this would even work. It was possible I'd kill Collin, and Kreturus would revert to his mass-less form and still live.

Glancing down at Collin, I noticed the smoothness of his cheek. His wounds were healed, and his skin looked as beautiful as it did the first day I saw him. With each breath I took, I prayed for another answer to come to me. There had to be another way. But, there wasn't. This *was* the prophecy. It said I killed Kreturus and became Queen of the Demons, ruler of the Underworld. This is where I would succeed or fail. This was the action that would define who I was at my core—good or evil. Could I sacrifice my soul mate to save the world?

My heart thundered in my ears and I couldn't stop shaking. Somehow the tooth was withdrawn from its hiding place and clutched firmly in my hand. I grasped it, ready to kill. Stab him and end this. End it now.

I'd like to say resolve shot up my spine with each breath I took, but it didn't. Doubt latched on, and I couldn't shake it. Losing Apryl nearly killed me, and I wasn't the one who killed her. I'd killed Valefar, and felt no regret, but this wasn't the same thing. The boy lying on the floor in front of me had part of my soul. I gave it to him.

Killing him would be like killing myself.

The poisoned fang hovered above his slowly breathing body, shaking in my hand. I wanted to touch my fingers to his sleeping face. I wanted to tell him that it had to be this way, that there were no other options. I wanted to hear his voice again, but I knew I couldn't. If he opened his startling blue eyes and spoke to me, I would lose my resolve. And I'd decided. I knew what I had to do. I knew how to end this.

I knew how to defeat Kreturus.

My jaw locked as I bit my bottom lip hard enough to taste my own blood. Straightening my spine, I drew every ounce of strength I could conjure. My muscles flexed.

I positioned the point of the silver tooth directly over *my* heart. And I swung. I swung as hard as I could. Every ounce of my being, every ounce of pain, every shattered dream, and every bit of misery that consumed me fueled that swing of the poisoned tooth. A scream erupted from my lips, as my arm came crashing towards my chest.

The prophecy would not be fulfilled.

Kreturus would not harness my power. He would not tempt me. He would not use love to twist me to his will.

The prophecy would die with me.

TORN

Book #3 in the Demon Kissed Series

Coming Winter 2011

CPSIA information can be obtained at www.ICGtesting.com
Printed in the USA
LVOW11s1549170815

450423LV00001B/23/P

9 780615 508276